BATTERED SOLES

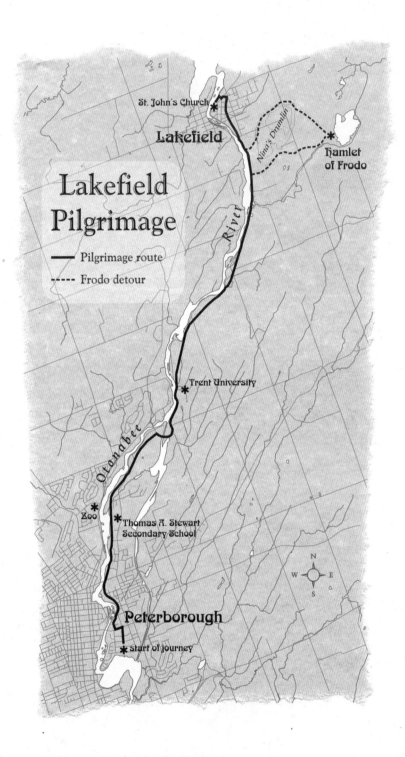

Lakefield Pilgrimage

—— Pilgrimage route

----- Frodo detour

St. John's Church

Lakefield

Nina's Drumlin

Hamlet of Frodo

River

Otonabee

Trent University

Zoo

Thomas A. Stewart Secondary School

Peterborough

start of journey

N
W E
S

to Stephan

with affection &
respect

BATTERED SOLES
Lakefield's Multicultural Pilgrimage

a novel by
Paul Nicholas Mason

Paul

TURNSTONE PRESS

Turnstone Press
Artspace Building
607-100 Arthur Street
Winnipeg, MB
R3B 1H3 Canada
www.TurnstonePress.com

Turnstone Press gratefully acknowledges the assistance of The Canada Council for the Arts, the Manitoba Arts Council, the Government of Canada through the Book Publishing Industry Development Program and the Government of Manitoba through the Department of Culture, Heritage and Tourism, Arts Branch, for our publishing activities.

 Canada Council for the Arts   Conseil des Arts du Canada   MANITOBA CONSEIL DES arts COUNCIL DU MANITOBA   Canadä

Cover design: Doowah Design
Interior design: Sharon Caseburg
Map: Weldon Hiebert   Map derived from Government of Canada National Topographic map # 31D/08 (1:50,000 series). © 2004 Produced under licence from Her Majesty the Queen in Right of Canada, with permission of Natural Resources Canada.

Printed and bound in Canada by Kromar Printing Ltd. for Turnstone Press.

Library and Archives Canada Cataloguing in Publication

Mason, Paul Nicholas
  Battered soles : Lakefield's multicultural pilgrimage / Paul Nicholas Mason.

ISBN 0-88801-305-1

I. Title.

PS8576.A85955B38 2005   C813'.54   C2005-900774-5

To Rachael and Nina—
And Annie, and Jackson and Molly:
Two streams, one river.

BATTERED SOLES

"But is it true?" asked Mother Bear.

"Some parts are true," said the Raven.

"Then which parts are made-up?" asked Little Bear.

"The parts which aren't fully true," said the Raven, and he flapped his wings noisily in hopes of changing the subject.

—From *Myth of the Troubadour Raven* by Andrea Drake

THE STATUE IN THE BASEMENT

THE SEEDS OF MY LAKEFIELD ADVENTURE WERE SOWN IN A Chapters bookstore in Toronto. I was leafing through a copy of Rosemary Mahoney's *The Singular Pilgrim: Travels on Sacred Ground*, when a grandmotherly lady in a mauve dress approached me. "That's a wonderful book," she said. "You should get that one."

"I think I will," I replied. "I like books about pilgrimages."

And so we chatted for a couple of minutes, about other books we had read, or hoped to read—but just as we were parting she startled me with a question. "Have you ever taken the Lakefield pilgrimage?"

"The what?" I said.

"The Lakefield pilgrimage," she repeated. "You walk from Peterborough to St. John's Church in Lakefield. There have been some remarkable healings there."

"Have there?" I said incredulously. It didn't seem likely to me. I did not then expect the miraculous to reveal itself on turf that was to some degree familiar.

I went to Trent University in Peterborough during the mid- to late-1970s, and took a degree in political studies. I'd come to know Lakefield then, at least a little, as a place where I'd cycle with a friend or two in the late spring or early fall to buy an ice-cream cone. We'd eat our cones on the lawn of the park near the cenotaph, enjoying the trees and flowerbeds and gossiping about our fellow students and courses and professors. It made for a pleasant excursion.

When I returned home from Chapters I placed a call to a former girlfriend, Louise, who moved to Peterborough a few years ago. We've remained friends and still chat every now and then, so she wasn't surprised to hear my voice. "I've told you about the pilgrimage, Paul," she said. "I know you're interested in that sort of thing."

"You've never mentioned it," I said indignantly. "I would have peppered you with questions if you had."

"It's those hallucinogens you took in your early twenties," said Louise. "You've fried all your memory circuits." She knew that would annoy me.

"You know very well that I've never *deliberately* ingested hallucinogens," I said, feeling a little miffed and hard done by. (But I have a story to tell on that front later in this narrative.)

Louise just laughed. "The pilgrimage is quite well known, and the route goes right by my house, on the Rotary Greenway Trail. There's pretty steady traffic through the summer. I'd guess that over six hundred people pass by on some Saturdays."

"What else can you tell me about it?"

"Not very much, I'm afraid. Why don't you call the minister at the Anglican church in Lakefield? I've heard him on the radio once or twice."

"The *Anglican* church?" I said. "Aren't pilgrimages more a Catholic thing?"

"I guess you'll find out," she said. "Drop by for tea if you decide to walk the trail."

It was easy enough to get the minister's number off the Internet, and a little later that evening I found myself calling Matthew

Deacon at home—though I wondered, fleetingly, if I shouldn't wait to try him during office hours. I confess that I've not had many conversations with Anglican priests, and this was the first I'd ever had by phone. I quickly got the sense that the Reverend Deacon was a bit bewildered by telephone technology. I imagined him holding the phone at arm's length—straining to hear and raising his voice to bridge the distance. He was perfectly gracious, however, and I learned a number of interesting details very quickly.

The focal point of the pilgrimage, he told me, is a piece of art in the basement of St. John the Apostle Church. It was executed by a Peterborough-based artist, Daz Tourbin, in 1996, and donated to St. John's. Daz, a woman in her late twenties, had been dating—here the Rev. Deacon's voice dropped to a confidential bellow—a younger *woman* who attended the Lakefield church, and Daz used to cycle along the Rotary Greenway Trail from Peterborough to visit her. In truth, the Rev. Deacon admitted, many senior members of the church were not terribly pleased with the gift. Daz had returned from a trip to India the previous year very much impressed with Hindu iconography, and the sculpture she donated to St. John's was a larger-than-life rendering of a blue-skinned Jesus playing the flute.

I interrupted him, asking, "Why was Jesus blue-skinned and playing the flute?"

"Because that's how *Krishna* is often portrayed in Hindu art," shouted the Rev. Deacon.

"Oh," I said.

Several days after Daz delivered the sculpture, and just as some fairly heated discussions over what to *do* with it began, the artist was knocked from her bike and killed in the south end of Peterborough (at the opposite end from the Lakefield side). That was very sad, of course, and it also had the effect of making it more difficult for people who hated the sculpture to say much against it; but their case was irreparably lost when, the day after the funeral, the church caretaker reported being cured of his arthritis while cleaning around the statue.

I asked, "Do you believe that?"

"Oh, yes." The good reverend seemed surprised by the question. "Harry had had terrible pain for years, and now he's bouncing around like a kangaroo. There's no question that he's been healed."

"But by the statue?" I persisted.

Rev. Deacon was silent for a moment. "I think I'd like to say that it was by the power of the Holy Spirit," he said finally.

"And there have been other healings since?" I asked.

"None that I can attest to absolutely," he replied cautiously (but still at top volume). "I don't know these other people as well as I know Harry, but they certainly *believe* they've been healed."

Apparently this all happened in the summer of 1996, and the church wardens took the fall, winter and following spring to decide how and when to display the sculpture. They eventually resolved, Solomon-like, to set it up in the basement of the church hall for two months during the summer—when the Sunday school, which met in the basement, was not in session. And so that's what they did ... and then, to their astonishment, on the first Saturday in July of 1997 a batch of pilgrims made the trek from Daz's former home in Peterborough, along the Rotary trail, to Lakefield. And the numbers have grown dramatically ever since, so that by the summer of 2003, when I resolved to pay my own visit, several thousands were expected to make the same journey over the course of two months. They would, Rev Deacon explained, set out from Peterborough any time between 8 a.m. and 4 p.m. on the Saturday or Sunday (though the numbers dropped off dramatically by noon on Sunday); most would stop at a few of the twenty-eight home altars or shrines that have sprung up along the route; many of them would stay in B & Bs, the campground, the new hotel, or some of the motels in Lakefield on Saturday night; and they would visit the church to see the statue at some point during the day on Sunday. People begin queuing up very early Sunday morning, he told me.

I was flabbergasted. "And what do you think of all this?" I asked.

Rev. Deacon paused. "I don't know," he said finally, his voice sounding normal for the first time. "It's all a bit unexpected. I'm still adjusting." He paused again. "God's ways are not ours," he said.

So I thanked him and said good-bye, and decided—after a brief consultation with Annie (my wife)—that I would walk the Lakefield pilgrimage route on the second weekend in July. And I began, from that moment, to look forward to the adventure with equal parts excitement and doubt.

But what made such an excursion interesting at all? It's certainly not as though I am, in any conventional sense, a religious person. My church attendance is, to be generous, sporadic, and I work in a thoroughly secular environment. And when I say that I'm not conventionally religious, I'm not hinting at some sort of New Age spirituality either. You're not going to catch me visiting sweat lodges, or kneeling at the feet of visiting gurus, or chanting mantras to the Earth Goddess. And yet, for all that, and as Louise's remark illustrates, I've long felt drawn to religious questions, even if I'm in short supply of doctrinal answers. Additionally, when I first heard about the healings in Lakefield, I was worried about my father, who had just experienced a couple of strokes. There's nothing like the ill health of someone you love to focus your mind on the big questions.

A little further research revealed that the pilgrimage route covered only about twenty kilometres, so it could be travelled comfortably in a single day, even allowing for stops at some of the twenty-eight shrines and home altars one encounters along the way. The fact that the pilgrimage was so self-contained and, frankly, short, appealed to me. I've visited a number of sacred sites over the years—Canterbury, Old Zimbabwe, Bouri-Bouri—and none of them had involved much of a walk. Something in me was drawn to the notion of setting time aside to make a journey, but I didn't (and don't) feel ready to take on El Camino de Santiago or Shikoku, or any of the several other long-haul pilgrimages. Partly that's a function of family responsibilities, limited vacation time, and limited resources. Partly it's the fact that I'm not sure of the benefits I would derive from taking a journey of that kind. Maybe it's just what I need to refresh myself spiritually. But I don't know that for certain.

In any event, I resolved to follow the pilgrimage route from Peterborough to Lakefield, and I planned to keep my mind as open as I could to the possibility that the journey might have value and meaning. And I promised Annie that I'd look after our children for a weekend later in the summer as a quid pro quo so she could attend an oil-painting workshop in Haliburton. And with these mental and logistical arrangements made, I boarded a Greyhound bus in downtown Toronto on Friday the 11th of July, 2003.

A LITTLE DOPE ON DAZ

LEAVING TORONTO ALWAYS LIFTS MY SPIRITS A LITTLE. IT'S NOT
that I dislike the city—Toronto's a fine place—but something in
me longs for spring-fed lakes and cathedral-like forests. Mind
you, after a few days away I always head back home with a
renewed appreciation for reliable plumbing, readable newspa-
pers and relatively few insects. Four summers ago, when Annie
and I took our honeymoon in the Picton area, we were mildly
bemused to find our hotel guide celebrating the resort's refusal
to use spidercides. "What a strange thing to advertise," said
Annie. We understood the implications a little better after we'd
spent half an hour in the room and counted six spiders on the
bedroom walls, and four spinning their webs in the bathroom.
Country folk seem to have a high tolerance threshold for sharing their living spaces with crawling creatures. Either that, or, as
in the case of our Picton hotel, they've recognised they're going
to lose the fight anyway and just thrown in the towel.

Be that as it may, I climbed on board the bus, found a seat
near the front, and hoped I'd have the next two hours to myself

for reading and sleeping. It's not that I'm rabidly anti-social, but you haven't anywhere to hide if your seatmate on a bus turns out to be a raving lunatic. In my university days, when I was regularly travelling back and forth between Kingston and Peterborough, I seemed to exert a magnetic attraction on aging female drunks and middle-aged men with halitosis and a pathological need to share their life stories.

But I was fated to have a seatmate, though he was a very pleasant young man with irreproachable breath. Ryan was a slim, blond fellow, and it took me only a few minutes to learn that he was gay, that he'd just come out to his family, that his mum was taking it well, that his dad was taking it poorly, that his younger brother was seriously embarrassed, that he'd had a 98% average in high school, that he was planning to study film and anthropology at university, that he wasn't in a relationship at the moment, that he still carried a torch for his first lover, and that he was crazy about *The Simpsons* and lemon meringue pie. Which was fine, all of it (though I was sorry about his dad and brother), but I swiftly discovered that he expected an equal degree of disclosure from me. "Well," I volunteered, "this is the first time I've visited Peterborough in about seven years." Ryan looked at me expectantly, and I briefly wondered whether I should fabricate something wildly interesting, but decided to stick with the truth. "I'm going on a pilgrimage," I added.

"From Peterborough?" said Ryan incredulously, and I was cheered to discover that I wasn't the only reasonably intelligent person in the province who'd never heard of the Lakefield pilgrimage. So of course I told him what I knew, and we talked about it a little, and then we somehow returned to the topic of Coming Out, so I just listened and nodded my head sympathetically and clucked my tongue from time to time. But I liked him, and I hope he's found someone as warm and engaging as he is, and that he's being Very Careful.

After a while Ryan fell asleep, and his head lolled over onto my shoulder. Twenty years ago I'd have been a bit uncomfortable about this, but the passage of time—the fact that I've grown up, and the fact that much of our society has grown up, too—made it easy simply to accept this involuntary intimacy. I looked out the window, and found myself thinking hard about my four years in Peterborough back in the 1970s. I remembered it as a rather depressed place then, but recognised that this might well represent a massive projection on my part. My last visit, seven years prior, had been very brief, but the place had been wreathed in fall colours, and I recall thinking that it looked cleaner and more interesting than it had in the seventies.

We'd left Toronto at 4.45 p.m., and pulled into the Simcoe Street terminal in Peterborough at 6.45—exactly two hours later. Ryan had come back to life as we began to stop for traffic lights. Our disembarking from the bus was hindered by the fact that a Very Large Man with many pieces of hand luggage insisted on getting off first. How he'd secreted all this hand luggage aboard in the first instance was a bit of a mystery—I'd only been allowed my fairly modest knapsack—but corpulent bullies will be served, and Mr Arbuckle (as I christened him) took his own sweet time. I composed my features into an expression of peace and patience, in the hope that the effect would, as it were, radiate inward. It didn't.

When it became clear that Mr Arbuckle's Berlin airlift would take a couple of minutes, I asked, "Do you need a hand?"

"This is expensive shit," he replied, scowling darkly at me.

"I'm good with shit," I said brightly, and I picked up a couple of his bags and raised my eyebrows meaningfully. We got off the bus together, though he kept casting suspicious glances over his shoulder, and seized the bags as soon as we hit the Tarmac.

In the terminal parking lot Ryan was met affectionately by a stocky young woman in jean shorts and pink running shoes. They went off in one direction, and I, after taking a moment to get my bearings, set off in another. I was heading for the Holiday Inn, where I was booked for the night, and knew that it was only a fifteen-minute walk from the terminal. It seemed to make sense to get a little exercise in advance of the rather more considerable exercise I'd be getting on the following day. And besides, I wanted a street-level view of my old home town.

Peterborough had changed, predictably enough, but some landmarks remained: the Salvation Army Temple was on the same street corner it was twenty-five years ago, just across the road from the Greyhound Bus Terminal (but the terminal itself is new). I found myself passing a number of new restaurants and shops on my way down Simcoe Street to George (the main drag), and on the whole things looked a bit more prosperous than they had. George Street itself was a mixed bag, however: yes, there were some familiar stores, and a few that seemed fancier than their predecessors, but there were also a number of empty and even boarded-up store fronts, and a surprising incidence of gang graffiti. Nor did I remember that there had been so many street people in the 1970s. In the several blocks I saw of George Street, I encountered three separate beggars. The first was an old man with a baseball cap and an empty liquor bottle in front of him; the second was a large and apparently mute aboriginal fellow; the third was a tattooed and bare-midriffed girl in army boots with a large German shepherd. In the spirit of religious pilgrimage I dropped a quarter in whatever receptacle was presented, and the old man and the native gentleman signalled their thanks—the native by smiling and spreading his hands in a kind of blessing. The tattooed girl, however, was unimpressed: "Well, that'll get me a dog biscuit!" she shouted after me. "I hope you enjoy it, then," I said, a little crossly, and carried on down the street, pursued by colourful obscenities.

I've stayed in a number of Holiday Inns over the years, and I do not despise them. Hot and cold running water, flush toilets, clean sheets and air conditioning are all excellent things. Yes, one usually finds more character in B & Bs and independent hotels, but one can also encounter cold showers, blocked toilets and triumphant spider colonies. At check-in I had my first encounter with other pilgrims. The people immediately in front of me were a tall, bearded man in his late twenties, and a lovely brunette of roughly the same age. I heard him ask the desk clerk if they had a special pilgrimage rate (the answer was no), so I addressed myself to his companion while that conversation unfolded.

I asked, "So you're also here to make the pilgrimage?"

"Yes, mostly," she said. "We've come down from Montreal." And then, with a little self-deprecating laugh, "I've never done anything like this before, but David has."

"How did you hear about it?"

"David used to live here, and he's done the walk. He knew Daz."

"Did he?" I said, at once surprised and pleased.

"They were good friends," she told me. At that moment David finished registering and turned around. He was a strikingly handsome man, and his handshake was firm but friendly. We all introduced ourselves, and I learned that the lovely brunette's name was Elizabeth. I tend to like Elizabeths.

I said, "So you knew Daz herself?"

"I did," said David. "We weren't exactly good friends," he added, "not intimates—"

"I hope not!" interrupted Elizabeth.

"—but we knew the same people, and went to the same parties, and we talked sometimes. I was at her last exhibition. She was a great lady."

"Is there any possibility that we could talk for a while later on?" I asked. "I don't want to interrogate you in the hotel lobby, but I'd love to hear a little more."

"Do you have dinner plans?" asked David.

"I don't want to trespass too much on your time together," I said, remembering how precious a weekend away with one's lover or spouse can be.

"It's okay," said David. "That's part of what this thing is about. Meeting people. Remembering someone special." So we made plans to meet up again in the lobby in about forty-five minutes, which, I calculated, should give them time for a quick boink and a shower.

A shower was uppermost in my own mind. I am not a small person, and I don't much like the heat. This hadn't been a particularly hot day, but I'd travelled on public transit, and had a bit of a walk, and I was more than ready for a stream of hot water.

After I'd unlocked the room, turned the air-conditioner to cold, and hung up the clothes in my luggage, I had a long shower. Whenever I shower in a hotel I'm reminded of a largely pleasant trip I made to Ireland in 1996 to see a play of mine performed. After Annie and I had booked into a hugely expensive independent hotel in Limerick I headed straight for the shower, only to find that there was no hot water. None. So I called the front desk to report the problem.

"It's not a problem, sir," said the front-desk manager. "We turn the hot water on at six."

"You turn the hot water on at six," I repeated, absolutely incredulous. "And how long is it on for?"

"Oh, it's on until nine," he said. "A good three hours."

"And then it goes off again," I deduced.

"That's right, sir. Until six in the morning."

Now, this may not come as a surprise to seasoned world travellers, and I would have accepted it with good grace had I been paying twenty dollars a night at a youth hostel, but the going rate here was ten times that amount and I felt thoroughly ripped off. "Does the electricity stay on all night?" I asked.

"Of course, sir," said the front-desk manager soothingly, as though he were calming a deranged psychiatric patient. But it didn't stay on. We had a power blackout at 9.16 p.m., and that, of course, played havoc with the hot water the following morning, and meant there was nothing but cereal and lukewarm milk for breakfast. I'd picked up something of the local attitude during our visit, however, and told Annie that if one looked closely enough into the cause of things, the English were surely to blame. (Any problem the Irish ever encounter is somehow the fault of the English. It's quite extraordinary. Mind you, if separatist agitators continue to poison political discourse in this country, and if that toxicity leads to rupture, we'll have an equivalent whipping boy of our own soon enough. And that will be unspeakably sad.)

So I have nothing nasty to say about the Peterborough Holiday Inn.

After my shower I dressed, read the hotel guide, looked out the window at the parking lot, tried to find CBC on the radio, fiddled with the television, then sat down to read a book until the full forty-five minutes had passed, whereupon I locked up and strode down the hall to the lobby. David and Elizabeth took an additional fifteen minutes, and arrived looking flushed in a healthy sort of way.

On the recommendation of the gentleman at the registration desk, we caught a cab to the Cringe Street Grill. We were greeted when we came in by a fellow who seemed to be doing an imitation of Uriah Heep (I mean the Charles Dickens character, not the rock band). He advanced on us wringing his hands and smiling in a sickly sort of way, before ushering us to our table. The restaurant itself was nicely decorated, but if Uriah had thrown us a little, the waitress who came to explain the menu and take our order positively set our teeth on edge: a slim, short woman with a pinched face and pursed lips, she radiated a potent combination of hostility and malevolence. And the food? Well, it was nicely prepared, but how often does one leave a North American restaurant hungry? My chicken breast dinner with rice and a vegetable medley covered about the same area as a Tim Hortons donut. Indeed, we all felt we'd have been better off going to Tim Hortons, and to this day I get hot under the collar when I remember what the bill came to.

But I digress. If the food portions were miserly and the service grotesque, the company was marvellous. David and Elizabeth were bright, vivacious people: they had done interesting things in their young lives, and they exuded warmth and good will. David was in the construction trades, with a particular interest in renovating old churches and schoolhouses, while Elizabeth worked as a translator for a Montreal publishing house. They laughed a lot, and they frequently touched each other—and they never made me feel like a third wheel.

"Daz was a passionate woman," David said. "She threw herself into everything she did. One year she had a huge thing for the Group of Seven, and she went up to Algonquin Park and stayed there for two months, painting every day. Then the next year she got excited about Monet and the Impressionists, and she did about twenty canvases in their style. And it was good work. It may not have been great, but it really was pretty good. I have two of her paintings myself.

"She was passionate about her friendships, too," he added. "She had many close friends, and quite a few lovers in the years that I knew her. And she wasn't exclusively lesbian. She went out with a guy, Brian Goth, for about two years, and they stayed really good friends. Daz was one of those really rare people who try always to see the good in others. I never heard her say anything nasty about anyone else."

"Do you know anything about her Lakefield lover?" I asked. It was clear that David saw nothing prurient about a discussion of this kind.

"I didn't know her," David said, "but I gather she's an artist, too. She makes beautiful silk scarves."

"You bought one for me," Elizabeth interjected.

"I did," said David. "You'll see a lot of them in Peterborough—and of course they're all one-offs, one-of-a-kinds."

And so we talked, and we had a drink or two, and when the food came we ate, briefly, and we were discussing the pilgrimage itself when the waitress came to see if we wanted dessert. David was just in the midst of talking about his hopes for the weekend. "I don't know how I feel about what's happened around her life," he said, "but I know that some good things have flowed from people meeting at the Lakefield church. I don't know if it has anything to do with God, but it feels like something good."

The waitress had been watching David's face while he said this, and she suddenly smiled in a way that I can only call malicious. "Are you going on that pilgrimage thing?" she asked.

"Yes," said David, giving her a genuine smile.

"You'll meet up with a lion before you find God in Lakefield," the waitress offered.

"I beg your pardon?" said David.

"Would you like some dessert?" asked the waitress. After a moment's silence we decided that we wouldn't, and we paid our bill and set out on foot for our hotel. But the waitress's unpleasantness had affected us all.

"Do you think they were a couple?" asked Elizabeth. "The maitre d' and the waitress, I mean."

"I'm sure they were," I said.

"I wonder where that kind of toxicity comes from," she said. I wondered, too.

As we approached the Holiday Inn we saw fireworks in the waterfront park a few blocks further on. David and Elizabeth opted to walk down to watch the display, but I had a phone call to make and some reading to do, so after a pleasant parting I went back into the hotel and to my room. My phone call made, I was briefly tempted by the array of adult films on offer via my television, but succumbing to their allure seemed subversive of the purpose of the weekend, so I climbed into bed with my copy of that indispensable guidebook *Lakefield Pilgrimage*. It told me that

> Peterborough, a blue-collar town of roughly 70,000, may seem an unlikely point of departure for any religious journey, but the city, like the pilgrimage, has many layers and dimensions. While the city is predominantly working class, it plays host to a university and a community college, and its many attractions include a first-class performance-space downtown, a fine zoo on the outskirts, a jewel of an art gallery on the shores of Little Lake, a number of accessible and attractive parks, and an impressive walking trail that traverses the city on the east side of the Otonabee River.

All this was true and encouraging, and I was in the process of putting our restaurant experience into its proper perspective when I heard a thumping noise in the hall. I lay listening to the noise for a couple of minutes, then got up, pulled my pants back on, and went outside to investigate. There, in the hall just a few yards down from my door, sat a woman in her mid-forties banging a shoe on the opposite wall. I watched her for a moment, but she seemed oblivious of me.

"Good evening," I said. "Is something wrong?"

The woman turned, and looked at me blearily. It was clear that she was very drunk. "Who the hell are you?" she said.

"I'm a guest at the hotel," I answered. "Do you need help of some kind?"

"What kind of help are you offering?" she said suggestively.

"Do you need help finding your room?" I asked.

"This is my room," she said.

"Would you like me to unlock it for you?" I offered.

The drunk lady thought about this for a moment, then shook her head from side to side. "No," she said. And then—apropos of nothing—"I'm pregnant."

"Oh," I said. "Congratulations."

"I don't want it," she said.

"I'm sorry to hear that," I said.

"Yeah," she said. "I really don't want it." She took a final vicious swipe at the wall with her shoe, then began struggling to her feet. I went to help her, but she waved me away. "Every time a man touches me I get pregnant," she said. She stood swaying for a moment, then made one final declaration: "If my baby is a boy . . . I'll puke." And with that, she coughed once—then vomited extravagantly against the wall.

I went back into my room and called the front desk. It was a long night.

THE BLESSING ON MARK STREET

THE TELEPHONE RANG WITH MY WAKE-UP CALL AT 7 A.M. IT seemed far too early. The Thumping Woman had left my head buzzing for some while after the Holiday Inn staff had prevailed upon her to go to bed, and I'd been awakened at 2.30ish by a couple of drunken men passing by, and talking about—of all things in July—the Toronto Maple Leafs. If anyone's even remotely interested, the Leafs' management doesn't know its ass from its elbow, and there are two guys from Kenora who would put the team on its feet in a season or two.

I stumbled into the shower, enjoyed copious quantities of driving hot water, then dressed in my hiking clothes. This wasn't the outfit I'd originally put together, mind you: I'd modelled that one for Annie, and she'd burst out laughing, so while I was having a little sulk in my study she'd made a few substitutions. I couldn't really see that my new outfit was a significant improvement, but I have to admit that no one roared with laughter at the mere sight of me all weekend, and that, certainly, is something to feel good about.

Breakfast is an important meal, especially if one's contemplating a walk of twenty kilometres. My most obvious choices were right across the road—the ubiquitous Tim Hortons, and a place called Smitty's. Like many Canadians, I've spent a great deal of money at Tim Hortons over the years, but I've never seen it as a breakfast sort of place. I headed off for Smitty's then, registering, as I entered into the morning sunlight, that it was already quite warm, and there wasn't a cloud in the sky.

The first and wonderful thing about Smitty's was that the waitresses weren't in the grip of demonic possession. This may seem a small thing, but after my experience of the previous evening I wasn't inclined to take it for granted. Most of the waitresses seemed to be rather robust women in their forties or fifties, though there were one or two dewy-eyed babes in their mid-thirties, one of whom had a waistline. I enjoyed a large and tasty serving of Belgian waffles with raspberries, at the end of which I had no waistline either. I would eat there again in a moment, and I join the editors of *Lakefield Pilgrimage* in recommending it to you. I particularly enjoyed the motherly black waitress who served the table next to me. Confronted by a mild expression of impatience from an elderly patron, she said, simply and musically, "Ah'm jes doin' the best ah can, honey"—and this disarmed him immediately, as it would have disarmed me, too. I confess I'm one of those men who like to be honeyed and sweetied: when I entered my first English pub, at the age of about thirty, I felt I'd come home when the waitress said to me, "What can I get you, luv?" It's silly, but there it is.

If there were any other pilgrims in Smitty's, I could not identify them, so there was no incentive to linger. I paid my bill, and headed for my temporary home across the street. Once there I visited the bathroom. There's a reason why I mention this: I have an utterly irrational horror of having to defecate outside. When I went to Trent I knew an outdoorsy sort of fellow—big beard, plaid shirt, a whiff of campfires about him—who once spoke rapturously, over a beer, of shitting in the woods. He told me that the best way to break down the barriers with a campmate was to take a crap with him under a canopy of trees. For the last twenty-five years I have neurotically feared that he's precisely the sort of man I'd run into if nature ever called at an inopportune moment. There I'd be, heading into the woods to do my solitary business, and suddenly, on a converging path, I'd spy a large, bearded, plaid-shirted fellow on a similar errand, and he'd call out, merrily, "Hey, let's"—well, you get the picture. I couldn't handle it. I'd have a nervous breakdown. Some barriers are fine with me. So I spent some time reading *The Globe and Mail*.

Returning from the restaurant the previous evening, I'd noticed that the Tourism Bureau was just north of my hotel, on the opposite side of the street. When I checked out of the Holiday Inn, I asked the taxi driver waiting outside to send a cab to pick me up there in about ten minutes. The bureau is a former train station with a sort of modified A-frame roof marking the entrance. Upon going in, I was greeted by a pretty young blonde, who flirted just enough to make a middle-aged man feel hoo, boy! I haven't lost it yet!—until he realised, after brief reflection, that the pretty blonde was roughly the same age as his oldest daughter, and he imagined blonde and daughter having a beer together and laughing about *this ancient bald guy who, like, was checking me out while I was working! It was so gross.* Middle-age is full of potential indignities of this sort. So I put on my sternest face, brusquely declined her offers of help, and contented myself with buying a couple of postcards and picking up a brand new coloured pamphlet about the pilgrimage route (complete with map). And then I went out to my cab, tripping over the doormat as I exited the building, and glumly aware that the blonde was stifling a laugh behind her command post at the counter.

I'm sure that cab-driving is a noble profession, and that it's full of balanced, hard-working, noble people who put in their twelve hours and go home to wives and children they treat with exquisite sensitivity. I'm sure of that. My problem is that my own experience with them radically defies the law of averages. I keep encountering the recently released convicts, the recently arrived

Al Qaeda trainees, the conspiracy theorists, and the frustrated opera stars. My all-time worst experience in a cab came in the sweltering summer of 1989 when a bear-like Italian gentleman alternated between singing Puccini arias and screaming abuse at Pakistanis as we sat, bumper-to-bumper, on the Don Valley Parkway, with a broken air-conditioner. It's mildly funny to remember it now, but it was hellish to live through.

This cab-driver, whose name I never learned, was a thin little man of about fifty, with a five o'clock shadow and a permanently mournful expression on his face. I had my first inkling as to his character when I remarked favourably on the new—to me—fountains in a park on Water Street. "I like them," I said. "I bet it's pleasant sitting on the benches, just watching and listening."

"Kids keep putting laundry detergent in them," said my driver dourly. "Makes an awful mess."

A half block later I tried again. The new Ministry of Natural Resources building is very attractively landscaped, with trees and shrubs in all sorts of imaginative places. "Well, that's nicely done," I said. "It's good to see real greenery against stone."

"Eats away at the foundations," said my driver. "Place won't last longer than a cat's fart."

And so it went: the new Galaxy Theatre—"Great to bring families to the downtown," I suggested provocatively—apparently causes appalling parking problems; the new Scotiabank—"Nice, clean design," I offered—employs far fewer people than the old Examiner building did. And the Quaker Oats factory, which is, for an industrial enterprise, remarkably sweet-smelling, well, it's likely to go bankrupt and move out of town any month now. It was a merry ride.

In any event, we crossed the Hunter Street bridge into East City, turned right on Mark Street, and suddenly, there we were, in front of the former home of Daz Tourbin. I paid Puddleglum—"Good day to get heat stroke," he ventured, by way of farewell—and I stepped out into a gathering crowd.

Daz's former home is a nice house on a nice street. It's a two-storey red brick, with white shutters up and down, and a small but serviceable front porch with a white railing. Once upon a time it would have been a single-family dwelling, but for the last fifteen years it's been divided into two apartments. Daz lived downstairs, at 112a, and her old apartment is now the home of Shelagh Korinsky, a good friend, apparently, who has made it her mission to help keep Daz's memory alive. To this end she has posted a sign on the front porch which reads, boldly and unequivocally, DAZ LIVED HERE! and she makes her front lawn available all day, every Saturday and Sunday in July and August, for the people who gather for a brief blessing before they embark on their walk. The *Lakefield Pilgrimage Guide*, to which I am indebted for this information, does not say whether she receives any financial consideration for this, but I'm inclined to doubt it. Certainly, there was no collection taken, and the vendors I saw (about whom more in a moment), professed themselves to be free agents. Nor have I any idea what the person or persons living upstairs at 112 Mark Street feel about things. I did speak with one neighbour, an older lady living two doors down, and she just shrugged when I asked whether the crowds bothered her. "You get used to it," she said. "They don't bother me. They're not noisy or anything."

When I arrived at 8.20 a.m. there were already over forty people assembled on the front lawn and sidewalk, and another forty gathered in the next ten minutes, many also coming by taxi or dropped off by private cars. The blessing is given every hour on the half hour between 8.30 a.m. and 4 p.m. Not everyone stays to be blessed—some are content with just seeing the house—but most, apparently, do wait for it. If we were eighty by the time everyone had assembled at 8.30, the numbers apparently swell to about one hundred and fifty by mid-morning.

So who was there, in the crowd, by 8.30? There were people of pretty well all ages, six through about seventy, though there were very few children—only four (I'd guess) under the age of sixteen. The bulk of us were probably middle-aged, though couples and individuals in their twenties and thirties could also be seen here and there. Racially speaking, the crowd was more

Toronto than Peterborough, by which I mean it was quite diverse. I was struck by the number of Asian Indians among us, fifteen or sixteen anyway, many of them in Hindu dress—but I had some idea why that should be so. *Lakefield Pilgrimage* contains the interesting information that the very first book about the pilgrimage was written in Hindi by a young religious scholar called Vikram Chandra. He gave a guest lecture (on transgressive sexualities) in the cultural studies department at Trent in the spring of 1999, and quickly became fascinated with what he heard about Daz's life and death, and the stories of healing that were coming out of St. John's. His seventy-eight-page guide was written over that summer and published, in Delhi, in the early winter. It sold an astonishing 322,000 copies over the next year, and is still in print.

I find it quite remarkable that nearly 350,000 subcontinent Indians should have been aware that Lakefield was a pilgrimage destination some years before the news swam into my own ken! But it bears mentioning, perhaps, that one often finds that a particular ethnic or racial group is drawn in disproportionate numbers to a sacred site far outside its normal territory. I gather that many of the people who flock to Marmora, Ontario are Filipinos, and even the guides at Bouri-Bouri are mystified by the numbers of Poles who make the journey.

At exactly 8.30 a modest Hyundai Accent pulled up in front of the house and out stepped a slim and rather pretty woman in her mid-thirties. This in itself was very welcome, but I soon realised that she was an Anglican priest—the priest, in fact, who was to give the blessing. She was greeted by several people in the crowd who seemed to know her, and after embracing a couple of them, and shaking hands with a few more, Jennifer made her way through the crowd and up onto the porch. One could be forgiven for not immediately realising she was a priest, because her vestments were not the ones you would expect: instead of black robes and a white collar, she wore a rainbow-coloured cloak. It was quite beautiful, but strikingly different from my notion of what an Anglican cleric would wear.

The crowd had become a bit more animated since her arrival. The bulk of us were still fairly quiet, but two vendors had come on the scene, and they wandered around trying to sell walking sticks. The sticks were rough-hewn things, but I was impressed with their heft and solidity. Their knobs—that's not quite the word I want, but it at least points you in the right direction— were carved with the likeness of a woman. "That's Daz," said one of the vendors, an unreconstructed hippie, by the looks (and scent) of him. "She did a self-portrait sculpture once, and our guy has copied it. They're all hand-rolled," he added—the Freudian slip suggesting that the bulge in his shirt pocket proba- bly wasn't a pack of Clorets. The stick cost me fifty dollars, but it struck me as a fine, home-grown souvenir. It may only be a mat- ter of time before Disney arrives, so who knows how much longer such things will be available?

The noisiest crowd-member, however, was a gangly fellow in his late twenties, with an oversized head and flood pants. He ran around the periphery of the crowd, poking the odd person and then exploding with laughter when they turned around. "I'm not getting paid for this, you know!" he shouted. And then, as another synapse fired randomly, "That's a nice hat!" He didn't seem to be under anyone's supervision, but he clearly didn't pose any sort of threat either, and people were wonderfully tolerant.

Jennifer raised her arms in a welcoming gesture and began to speak. "My friends," she said, "I welcome you in the name of the Father, and of the Son, and of the Holy Spirit. And I welcome you also in the name of the God who created all of us, and loves all of us, and watches over us all." ("Look at me, God!" cried the gangly fellow. People laughed.)

"You are about to undertake a journey," said Jennifer, "that some of you make out of curiosity, and some perhaps simply for exercise. I would ask you to remember, though, that some here today will make this walk in the hope of finding healing for bod- ily or spiritual hurts. The church cannot guarantee such healing, but I hope you may find it if indeed you seek it. And I hope the walk will be meaningful for you, whatever expectations you may bring to it. I invite you now to bow your heads in prayer." (Most people did.)

"Almighty God," Jennifer prayed, "make clean our hearts within us, and help us to seek and to find only those things that will be pleasing in your sight. Bless us all, dear Lord, and may we grow stronger in the knowledge of your love with every step we take. Amen."

Most people echoed her amen, and a good number of folk crossed themselves, suggesting that there was a fairly sizable Catholic contingent among us. "This morning," said Jennifer, "I'm going to take you by the Driscoll Terrace route. Some of you may wish to go by way of the Rotary Greenway Trail directly off Mark Street, and I'll certainly point that out to you. Like the Kingdom of Heaven," she smiled, "everyone gets to the same place in the end." I rather liked that, and my reading of the previous evening meant that I also knew what she was talking about.

Some would say that the most logical and direct route from Peterborough to Lakefield is to walk down Mark to Hunter, take a brief jog right on Hunter, and then enter the Trail at one of its most obvious gateways on the left-hand side. There's no question that Daz herself often took this route when she cycled to Lakefield. There's equally no question that Daz sometimes turned left on Hunter, stayed on the street for about a block, then turned right onto Driscoll Terrace. When Driscoll Terrace starts to bear right there's what used to be a simple footpath, and after a few hundred yards that footpath intersects with the Rotary Greenway Trail. It may seem a tiny thing to be arguing about, but the residents of Driscoll Terrace felt so strongly that their street was the right approach that in the year 2000 they launched a fund-raising campaign to build a special arch over the start of the footpath. Additionally, and not surprisingly, there are two home altars open to the public on Driscoll Terrace. Neither of them is recommended by the guidebook, but the description of one of them had piqued my curiosity. I resolved, then, to follow Jennifer, and let the *formalists* (as Vikram Chandra called them) take the more direct route.

So we set out on foot, of course, enjoying the sun but already, some of us, a bit concerned about how hot it would be later on. Mark Street was nicely shaded by trees, however, so the first part of the walk was very easy. People chatted comfortably in their already existing configurations, and the inevitable elongation of the line began, the youngest and the fittest coming to the fore, and the older or less fit falling to the rear. While far from being the most fit in the group, I quickly caught up to Jennifer, and walked beside her for a couple of minutes. I asked her whether she believed in the healings.

"I honestly don't know," she answered. "I've met the caretaker at St. John's, and he seems a very honest man, but I don't know what his health was like before he claims to have been healed. On the other hand," she said, "I know a man called William, a gay member of my own parish, and he was very sick when he came down here, and went into instant remission after taking the walk. Now, what is that? Power of suggestion? Mind over matter? Coincidence? Or the Holy Spirit at work? I'd like to believe it's the Holy Spirit. William believes that."

"Do you see any potential for harm?" I asked.

"No. I'm not thrilled about the merchandising," she said, with a nod at my stick, "but it's not crassly commercial, and to this point it's been quite respectful. And the church is not making grandiose claims about this, you realise. We bless pilgrims, and we welcome them at the other end, at the church itself, but we don't make promises or representations, and we don't charge them for anything." She paused. "Some people's lives genuinely seem to change for the better after taking this walk," she said, "and I've never known anyone hurt by it. At the very least, people take several hours to get out in God's creation and enjoy the trees and birds and flowers. And most people will make a friend or two."

I thanked her for her time and, recognising that there were others who wanted to speak with her, I dropped back a little and thought carefully about what she'd said. It made good sense to me, and I found myself liking her very much. I think I'd cheerfully attend a church she led.

When we came to Hunter Street, Jennifer stood at the cross-roads directing people left or right depending on what route they wished to take. I turned left, then stopped briefly to look at Mark Street United Church (the Rev. Dr. Root presiding), and so was passed by a number of folk. Part of the church reminded me, architecturally, of a school I attended in British Columbia, and I found myself transported back to third grade, playing soccer and tether ball in the shadow of Capitol Hill in Burnaby. What does it mean, I wondered, when a church doesn't look like a church—when it resembles a bank building or a ski chalet or, indeed, a school? On the other hand, the very phrasing of the question reveals that I have a predetermined notion of what a church should look like, and that image is certainly conditioned by my experience rather than by divine direction. A professor of mine once suggested that church buildings reflect the prevailing ideology of the time, but I'm by no means confident that that's true. It strikes me as too neat a generalisation.

So what should a church look like? Honesty compels me to admit that my own ideas are fairly conventional. I do like the notion that some part of a church should, as it were, point up, that feature serving as a metaphor for transcendence. I also believe that a church should be built in such a way that external noise is at least muted and ideally silenced: we need silent places if we are ever to hear the still, small voice in which, the Bible tells us, God sometimes speaks. If I had the design of a church, it would be surrounded by gardens—and there'd be a pond and a waterfall outside. Actually, this is a subject on which I'm not at all doctrinaire: beauty comes in all sorts of forms, and the one absolute prerequisite for a church, it seems to me, is that it should be beautiful, even if that beauty is beautifully simple, Zen-like.

I turned to move on down Hunter, and saw immediately in front of me a reasonably tall and rather heavy fellow wearing, of all things on a summer's day, a leather jacket with the words CHICAGO CORONER'S OFFICE splashed across the back.

ERNIE AND THE SOUP

ONE OF MY BEST FRIENDS IN ALL THE WORLD OWNS A JACKET with the words L.A. FIRE DEPARTMENT emblazoned on the back, even though he is neither a fireman nor, for the matter, from Los Angeles. He's quite forthright about his sartorial choice, however: "It helps me pick up chicks," he told me once. I can see that. I can see that there might be something romantic about fire-fighting. But I'm not sure I'd want anything to do with the kind of woman who would be excited by someone simply because he works in a coroner's office: there is, after all, some distance between saving lives and dissecting corpses. And in saying this, of course, I reveal an abysmal ignorance about coroners, who are probably the sexiest forensic investigators on the planet.

Be that as it may, while I was still deliberating whether to speed up and chat with this large gentleman in the coroner's jacket, a car filled with teenage boys came alongside us, and a particularly greasy specimen poked his head out the window and yelled, "Go home, you bunch of wacko religious freaks!" at the line of pilgrims.

The gentleman in the coroner's jacket didn't even pause to take breath. He let rip with the most violent, imaginative, colourful stream of profanity I've heard on three continents. It touched upon the boys' ancestry, their mental acuity, the things they'd likely done with barnyard animals, and their mothers' notions of hygiene. "Ya bunch of shit-eating, piss-drinking sons of goat-humping whores," he began—and then he got really creative. It was a virtuoso performance, and it absolutely silenced the boys in the car. They sped off.

Many of the pilgrims had stopped in their tracks to listen, and they stared at the fellow in the coroner's jacket, some disbelieving, some horrified, some frankly impressed. "Sorry, folks," said the coroner's man, and he waved at the crowd. And then, seeing me behind him, and recognising that I was in the ranks of the impressed, he stuck out his hand and said, "Hi, I'm Ernie." And that is how I met Ernie Gold.

Ernie is so colourful a character in his professional life that I've had to fiddle with his name, and engage in some creative misdirection when it comes to his home turf. He's a twenty-first-century character of Dickensian stature who, alas, does not have a Dickens as his Boswell. He deserves one: I will have to serve. He was, as I've already said, a large man: he probably weighed about 270 lbs, distributed on a six-foot frame. His face was fleshy, and he had a bit of a gut, but you wouldn't call him fat. A big guy. A big personality.

We fell into step as we walked down Hunter Street, and Ernie confided that he was from the Kitchener (Ontario) area, that he had a wife and three children, that he collected paraphernalia from the American Civil War, and that he thought there was a world-wide conspiracy of liberals and feminists to destroy western civilisation. He was, he said, deeply concerned about the erosion of Christian family values. I enjoy characters, and I particularly enjoy characters who embody contradictions of one kind or another. Ernie's faith seemed to me at least a little at odds with his extraordinary command of profanity, but this was only the beginning. "What do you do for a living, Ernie?" I asked him.

"I drive for an agency," he said.

"What kind of an agency?" I asked.

"An escort agency," he said cheerfully.

And that piece of his story came out over the course of the next few moments, confirming for me that our culture encourages the most astonishing level of self-disclosure to strangers. (Not that we remained strangers: we became good friends over the course of that weekend.) Ernie worked, he told me, for a particular agency in the Kitchener area. He would come on duty at about 6 p.m., when he turned on his business-specific cell phone. Regular clients and travelling businessmen would call the agency, hear what girls were on duty that evening, choose one from the descriptions, then be told to have a drink and relax for the next fifteen minutes. The agency dispatcher would then call Ernie on his cell, and direct him to pick up girl A and deliver her to hotel Y. The girl, meanwhile, would have received her own phone call, and would freshen up and await Ernie's arrival.

I asked, "Who are these girls?"

"Single moms," said Ernie. "College students. Housewives with a drug habit. Girls with financial problems."

Ernie would deliver the girl to the hotel where her client was staying, and wait a few minutes while she went in. If the client's door opened on to the parking lot, he'd be told to unlock it for her. If that wasn't the case, she'd go in by the front door and sail past the hotel's front desk. Front desk workers usually look the other way, Ernie told me.

When the girl arrived at the client's room, she'd make a quick assessment, then place a call back to the agency. If she didn't feel comfortable she'd use a code word, and the dispatcher would immediately ring Ernie and tell him to get up there as fast as possible. Usually, however, there wasn't a problem, and the girl would get on with the business of negotiating the *service*, for which she always required payment in advance.

There's something in me that's fascinated by the life of the demimonde, even if a mix of things—the fact that I love my wife and family, a horror of disease, and a profound disinclination to get arrested—prevent me from diving into it. The fascination kept me asking the odd question and listening carefully to the answers. That part of me that refuses to surrender completely to prurience had a different kind of question, however, and I eventually found the space to put it: "Why are you on this pilgrimage, Ernie?"

Ernie thought about the question for a moment. "Sometimes I lie in bed at four in the morning and I ask myself what I'd say to Jesus if he called me right then," he said at length. "Right now I don't know what I'd say. This seemed like a good time to think about it."

We had by this time rounded the corner onto Driscoll Terrace, and just a little way down the road could see, on the right-hand side, a number of two-storey yellow brick buildings. These buildings were in fact row houses, with three separate residences per building. Their front doors were not level with the street, meaning that one had to climb five steps to enter any one of them. I pulled out my guidebook and flipped it open to the section which gave the locations and descriptions of the home altars. "Are you interested in going in?" I asked Ernie.

"In where?" asked Ernie. So I explained that this wasn't just a walk with a single destination, but that there was the opportunity to visit a number of homes along the way and see the shrines and altars their owners had created.

"There are altars in this dump?" asked Ernie sceptically.

"Yes," I said, and showed him the description that had piqued my own curiosity.

> The first shrine on the Driscoll Terrace route is at number 346. Created and maintained by Mr and Mrs Bill Krupp, the altar consists of a large table covered in a dark green tablecloth. Mrs Krupp has sewn strips of material meant to represent roads all over the tablecloth, and Mr Krupp has placed postcard-size reproductions of some of Daz Tourbin's paintings in the corner of the intersections made by the criss-crossing road network. To reinforce the notion that these strips of material are

indeed roads, Mr Krupp has also positioned his impressive collection of Dinky Toy models of London buses at various points along them. In the middle of the display is a large bowl aquarium filled with yellow tropical fish. A crucifix is anchored in the sand at the bottom of the bowl.
Rating: ★

Ernie read this very carefully. "Are these people crazy?"

"I've no idea," I said.

"What does the star mean?"

"Well," I said, "it's one star out of a possible *five*. It's a pretty low rating."

"And you want to go in there," said Ernie. It was a statement rather than a question.

"I'm curious," I said.

Ernie sighed. "All right," he said. We climbed the steps and knocked on the door. A moment later it was opened by a fairly short, cross-looking woman in her early sixties. She wore a dress with a subdued floral print, and she smelled vaguely of mothballs.

"Yes?" she said.

"We've come to see your altar," I said.

"What?" she said. She was clearly hard of hearing.

"We've come to see your altar," I repeated, enunciating each word very clearly.

"You want some *water*?" she said, amazed that we should disturb her for so paltry a reason. Ernie snorted.

A stooped gentleman in his mid-sixties appeared behind her. "They've come to see the *shrine*, Dolly," he said.

"Why didn't he say so?" she said, glaring at me as if I'd just tried to sell her a bag of rotten bananas.

"She's a little agitated today," said Mr Krupp as he ushered us in. "It's the heat." If the outside was heating up fast, the inside of the Krupp home was already hot and humid. One had the sense that it hadn't lost any of the previous day's heat. It didn't help matters that something was obviously cooking: we could smell something richly meaty. At the end of a long day chopping wood in the cold, it would probably have smelled good. As it was, at the beginning of a hot summer's morning, it was a bit much. "I'm just making some soup," said Mr Krupp, leading us through the tiny kitchen, past the bubbling saucepan, and up a steep flight of stairs. Mrs Krupp, meanwhile, had gone back to the television in a small sitting room just off the kitchen. The blare of a game show receded a little as we climbed the stairs.

There were two bedrooms and a bathroom at the top of the stairs. One of the bedrooms, however, had been transformed into the Krupp shrine, and there, just as the *Guide* promised, was a large table (almost filling the room), covered by a dark green tablecloth. Mrs Krupp's *roads* were not skillfully sewn on, but at some point since the *Guide* had been published—and perhaps in response to it—someone had painted shaky dotted yellow lines down the middle of the strips of black material. The buses were there, and so were the postcards, but the bowl aquarium filled with yellow fish and a crucifix dominated the landscape. Ernie and I stared at the scene for a moment: we'd neither of us seen anything quite like it before. Mr Krupp watched us anxiously. "Do you like it?" he asked.

Ernie cleared his throat. "What's with the fish?" he asked.

"What's that?" said Mr Krupp.

"Do the fish have any symbolic significance, Mr Krupp?" I asked, eager not to give offence.

"No," said Mr Krupp. "They're just fish."

"Nice-looking fish," I said helpfully. "Aren't they, Ernie?"

"They're piss yellow," said Ernie.

"They contrast nicely with the green of the tablecloth," I said, looking daggers at my large companion. "This is very fine, Mr Krupp."

"I'm glad you like it," said Mr Krupp.

"Yes," I said, "we're very impressed. Aren't we, Ernie?"

"I like the Hot Wheels," said Ernie.

"The what?" said Mr Krupp.

"He means the buses," I said quickly. "The buses give the whole thing a really, um—" but in truth I couldn't see what the buses did for the display as a whole, so I coughed extravagantly. I suspected then, and now know for a fact, that Daz had never visited England. The toys were important to Mr Krupp, however, and perhaps that was reason enough to include them. We stood and gazed at the shrine for a while longer.

After a couple of minutes Mr Krupp said, "Would you like some soup?"

I was about to say *no, thank you, we really should be getting along,* but Ernie got in first. "Sure," he said. So we filed downstairs and Mr Krupp pulled two bowls out of the cupboard and ladled generous helpings of thick, meaty soup into each of them, then placed them on the tiny kitchen table. Ernie and I sat down, and Ernie tucked into his serving with enormous enthusiasm. My breakfast was still very much with me, so I addressed myself to the meal—and it was a *meal*—rather more timidly.

"This is good," said Ernie, smacking his lips loudly. "What's the meat?"

Mr Krupp beamed: he was clearly as proud of his soup as he was of his shrine. "Beef, lamb, pork sausage, turkey and some salmon," he said. "Whenever we have a meal I boil the bones and add the stock to the pot."

Suddenly I felt quite sick. I'm not a dedicated meat eater at the best of times, and the thought of several months' worth of carcass leavings stirred up together with a bit of onion, carrot and rice made me long to be anywhere other than sitting at that table. "Could I have a glass of water, please?" I said. And that, of course, was the moment Dolly chose to enter the room. She looked at me darkly, with the air of a woman whose every worst suspicion has just been confirmed.

I'll draw a discreet veil over much of the rest of the visit. Mr Krupp was good enough to leave the room briefly, giving me the opening I needed to offer Ernie my almost untouched bowl of soup. Mrs Krupp, meanwhile, stood by the kitchen window, fanning herself with a magazine and watching every move I made. Shortly after the exchange of bowls she made a most horrendous noise—a noise that made the hair on my neck stand on end—

then spat viciously into the sink. I was immoderately grateful when Mr Krupp returned.

As we were leaving I tried to pay for the food, but Mr Krupp would have none of it. "You are my guests," he said graciously. "Thank you for coming to see the Krupp shrine." We shook hands and started down the steps.

But our visit was not quite over. While everyone else who had taken the Driscoll Terrace route had passed this house by (whether discouraged by the review in the *Guide* or simply eager to get on the trail proper I honestly don't know), one other person clearly wanted to visit. He was a thin and rather sad-looking gentleman in his early forties, and he was confined to a wheelchair. It was a self-propelling wheelchair, and there was no one with him. "How do I get in?" he asked.

Mr Krupp seemed a bit taken aback. "Do you need help getting out of the wheelchair?" he said.

"I have to stay in the chair," the gentleman replied. "Where's the ramp?"

"There isn't a ramp," said Mr Krupp. "You have to come up by the stairs, and the shrine's on the second floor."

"There *should* be a ramp or an elevator," said the fellow in the wheelchair. "All public facilities should have access for people with disabilities." Mr Krupp looked lost.

Some problems simply don't have remedies. Mr and Mrs Krupp were in no position to afford to install a wheelchair ramp. They were not wealthy people, and while they had opened their home to the public, it was still very much a private residence. "Could we possibly lift—" I began to say, but the disabled gentleman had already, with a look of anger and distress, backed away from the house, and begun to wheel himself down Driscoll Terrace.

Mr Krupp was silent. We could see that he was deeply embarrassed. Ernie clapped him on the back: "Guy's got a pickle up his arse," he said helpfully. "Great soup," he added.

"And the shrine was really *memorable*," I said. (And it was, you know.) So we negotiated the steps and set off down Driscoll Terrace, Ernie burping contentedly, and I still feeling a bit queasy and wishing I had stowed four bottles of water in my knapsack rather than two, at least in part because it was obvious that Ernie had brought nothing at all, and it was already hot.

After a couple of minutes of brisk walking we could see the archway over the trail entrance. When first I read about it, I imagined a very much smaller-scale version of the Arc de Triomphe in Paris, but this was more like the kind of arch or gate you see at the entrance to parking lots at some Chinese restaurants. As we drew nearer we could see that it was made of wood, but had been painted in garish green and red. The oriental flavour was somehow reinforced by the animal sculptures that stood on either side of the arch keeping guard. These were original Tourbins, I knew, and Ernie and I were both impressed with their artistry. On the left there was a grizzly bear, and on the right—a penguin. They made an odd pair, but the effect was friendly.

Jennifer, the Anglican minister, was standing patiently next to the penguin. She spoke briefly to the fellow in the wheelchair as he went through, then greeted us as we came up. "You're the last in this group, then," she said. "What did you think of the Krupps' shrine?"

"It was pretty weird," said Ernie, "but he makes a great soup."

"You *ate* it?" said Jennifer.

"Two bowls," said Ernie contentedly. "Are you going to walk with us?"

"No," said Jennifer. "I must go back to give the next blessing. I'm on duty until 12.30. Would you like to be anointed?" She was holding a small bottle of oil.

I suspect that Ernie would cheerfully have drizzled the oil over a slice of pizza, but the thought of having it on his forehead clearly alarmed him. It seemed a charming thought to me, however, and I leaned forward for Jennifer to make the sign of the cross. Touch is a funny thing. The accidental touch of an attractive stranger can be sexually electric: most of us would admit that. The deliberate touch of a kind and loving person can also be very powerful, and I was astonished by the sense of well-being

Jennifer's brief touch bestowed. It made me wonder, too—not then, but weeks later—whether part of Jesus of Nazareth's healing power derived simply from his willingness to touch people who had not been touched gently for years. A kind word; a gentle touch: who can put a value on these things?

A little sidebar story. For some years I took a week every summer to attend a theatre school at a Canadian university. It was a kind of holiday. In 1994 I found myself in a course called Creating a Character, taught by a lovely lady called Heather. Heather had plenty of experience and some wonderful ideas; she was also very patient. I liked and respected her, and so did most of my classmates. One of our classmates, however, was a tiny older woman I'm going to call Golda. Golda had worked as a professional actress for some decades, though how regularly and with what success I did not—and do not—know. Golda was an *angry* woman: her anger was apparent as soon as one met her. One had the sense of a brooding presence, a volatile mix of grievance and outrage.

I was one of the early targets of Golda's disfavour. Heather had subdivided the class and assigned us scenes, and I found myself with a fellow called Al playing a scene from Pinter's "The Caretaker." Al and I did a good job with the scene: we found its sinister quality, made its inherent nastiness explicit. I did something horrible with a piece of string that struck people as fairly chilling. It worked: we got a nice round of applause and sat down flushed with our success.

Golda, however, was unimpressed. She sidled up to me during the tea break as I was stirring sugar into my cup. "You got some nice applause in there," she said.

"Yes," I said. "People seemed to like it."

"You are feeling good?" she said.

"I'm feeling great," I said. "You know, this has given me the confidence—"

"Paul Mason," she said, "I will tell you somethingk. Those people in there, they are fools. They know *nothingk*. The teacher knows *nothingk*. You and I," she said, "You and I know that what you did in there was *shtick*. Just *shtick*. You can fool them, maybe," she said, "but you can't fool me, and I don't think you are so stupid you can fool yourself."

"Oh," I said.

"So the next time you are lookingk in the mirror, Paul Mason," she said, "You look deep into your eyes and say to yourself, 'No more *shtick*.' Hmm? Then one day—one day—you will do good work. Maybe." So of course I was incredibly deflated and spent the next two days second-guessing myself every time I got up to try something new. But Golda was simply warming up with me: she took on Heather, our teacher, later that very afternoon. Heather had introduced an exercise—what it was I don't now remember—and Golda didn't like it. "This exercise is for shit," she announced.

"I beg your pardon?" said Heather, at once startled and polite.

"This exercise is for shit," Golda repeated. "This course is for shit. Your teaching is for shit. You know *nothingk*—nothingk about the theatre. You are a very stupid woman!" And she stormed out.

To her great credit, Heather picked up the pieces and helped create a stimulating and memorable week for all of us—though Golda, by her own choice, did not return to the class. But Golda did not leave the school. She had paid her fees, and she was determined to take advantage of the meals, the movement and voice sessions, and the opportunity to intimidate anyone she came across. A number of people would have Golda stories by the end of the week.

On the Saturday of the week, the last full day, Heather's group met with the beautiful movement teacher for the last time. I don't remember her name, but the men had taken to calling her The Goddess. We went through a series of exercises, then The Goddess asked us to find a partner. I looked around and, as luck would have it, there was Golda—with everyone else moving rapidly away from her. "Oh, *damnation*," I said to myself—those weren't my precise words—and I made my way towards her, smiling feebly, my ears flattened back, my tail wagging pathetically.

Now the exercise was fairly simple. It involved one partner lying flat on her back, and her partner kneeling behind her head, supporting her head in his hands, raising it very gently, cradling it, then lowering it carefully to the floor. I did so. Golda was very tense at first, but as the process unfolded she began to relax, and by the end of the three minutes the exercise took she was completely limp. And weeping.

"Are you all right, Golda?" I asked.

"Yes, yes, I'm all right," she said, wiping her tears away. "Your acting is full of shtick, Paul Mason," she said, "but you have very gentle hands. Do you know how long it's been since someone touched me gently?" she said.

"No, I don't, Golda," I answered.

"Twenty-five years," she said—then she embraced me, and fled the class.

The point I'm trying to make—and to illustrate—is that another person's touch can be profoundly healing. On that front, I'm indisputably fortunate: I have been touched gently every day of my life by mother or lover or wife or friends or children, and as a consequence, surely, I have little desire to lift a hand against anyone. Anyway, Ernie and I took our leave from Jennifer, and strode through the gate. And we continued on our way, sweating by now, admiring the sumac and the Queen Anne's Lace, until we saw something that caused my friend Ernie great excitement.

THE CAT LADY

TWO WOMEN KISSING. ERNIE AND I WERE TRAMPING ALONG, AS I say, admiring the shrubs and flowers in the foreground, when we turned a bend in the footpath and there, right before our eyes, were two beautiful young women kissing. It took us a moment to be sure that was indeed the case—that one of the two wasn't a young man with an unusual haircut—but when we were sure, Ernie exhibited the same degree of enthusiasm he had already displayed over Bill Krupp's soup. "Lesbians!" he cried happily.

"Shut up, Ernie!" I hissed—but the two ladies had heard. Fortunately, and thank God for their forbearance, they laughed.

"That's right," said one of them. "But that's not usually how we introduce ourselves. I'm Emily, and this is Ruth."

So we shook hands, and Ernie demonstrated that he could observe the social niceties and leer at the same time, which takes some doing. I asked, "Are you on the pilgrimage, or just out for a walk?"

"Oh, we're on the pilgrimage," said Emily. She was a red-haired woman of about nineteen, and she wore hiking shorts and a Greenpeace T-shirt. "We just stopped to adjust our knapsacks and have a quick snog."

"Don't let us stop you," said Ernie, his leer growing more pronounced.

"You're a dirty bird, aren't you?" said Ruth, but her tone was not confrontational. She was the same age as Emily but clad in a light summer dress, and her complexion and eyes reminded me of photographs I've seen of Romany people—gypsies.

"Ernie's from Kitchener," I said, vaguely hoping this would excuse him. "We'll leave you to it, then," I added.

"Unless you need a hand," said Ernie cheerfully—but he yielded when I pulled him forward. "See you later, ladies," he called back to them.

"Ernie," I said, when we had moved on fifty yards or so, "you can't leer at women like that."

"Why not?" said Ernie.

"Because they might be offended."

"They weren't offended," said Ernie reasonably. "I love lesbians," he added. "The pretty ones, I mean. Not the ones with hairy legs and double chins." I groaned, but Ernie was oblivious, and we were both swiftly distracted as we now found ourselves leaving the Driscoll Terrace footpath and joining the Rotary Greenway Trail. The spot was marked, rather disconcertingly, by a small totem pole. We stopped to look at it, and to read the brass plaque at its base:

> In honour of Daz Tourbin (1966-1996). Erected by
> the All-People's Association of the Anishanabee.
> "The Great Spirit loves us, every one."

"What do you suppose this All-People's Association is?" asked Ernie.

Now, I attended Trent University in the late 1970s, and in those days the homophile association on campus used to hold All-People's dances—dances at which homosexuals *and* heterosexuals were welcome—so I hazarded a guess that the APAA was a gay and lesbian native group. Ernie thought about this for a moment, then asked a penetrating question. "Does this mean Daz is some kind of lesbian saint?"

"I certainly don't think she's *simply* that," I said, "but she may be that as well as a number of other things to other people." It was an interesting thought: it seems likely that none of the various popes has ever canonised someone who was known to be homosexual. But in just the same way that the absence of a female principle (or principal) in the Holy Trinity of Father, Son and Holy Ghost caused simple Catholics to begin worshipping Mary, one sees how the absence of a gay or lesbian saint might cause faithful homosexual folk to want a saint made in their own image. I shared this inspiration with Ernie, and he thought about it for a moment or two.

"God, it's getting hot," he said, and we moved on.

The Rotary Greenway Trail runs roughly parallel to the Otonabee River in Peterborough's East City. It follows the route taken by old railway lines. At some points along it, even while you're still in the city, you see nothing but bushes and trees. At other points, you look into the front or back yards of houses that abut the trail. In some places you find yourself gazing at apartment buildings and even institutions like schools. In this, the early part of our walk, we were seeing lots of houses, and our attention was caught by a modest little place whose back yard was festooned with Tibetan prayer flags.

"Is there a shrine in this house?" Ernie asked.

I didn't think so, but I consulted the *Guide* just in case. "No," I said, "but there's one just a little further on if you want to stop again."

"What does the *Guide* say about it?" asked Ernie. I read aloud,

The Domm home altar (the second on the Rotary Greenway route) was created by Roxy Domm, and appears to be a celebration of her several cats. The altar itself occupies a prominent position in her living room, and is made of an old-fashioned writing desk on which Ms Domm has

> placed small porcelain models of cats in a variety of typ-
> ical feline poses. On either side of the writing desk, addi-
> tionally, there are posters of cats by prominent local
> artist Richard Hayman, who was a good friend of Daz
> Tourbin. Ms Domm has built an interactive element into
> her altar, as she has placed her own cats' food dishes at
> the base of the desk. There is no clear religious symbol-
> ism on the altar, but when asked about this Ms Domm
> reminded the questioner that cats themselves were wor-
> shipped in Ancient Egypt. Rating: ★

"What's the rating on that one?" asked Ernie. I told him. "Does it say anything about soup?" he added hopefully.

"No, I said. "Would you like to skip it?" I confess that I wanted to. I'd noticed that the *Guide* awarded several shrines a full five stars, and I was reluctant to devote too much time to also-rans, no matter how worthy or well-intentioned.

"No, let's give it a try," said Ernie. "I like cats."

"All right," I said. "Be on the lookout for a small house with red vinyl siding and a sign saying DOMM." And we pressed on.

It didn't surprise me when, a few moments later, Ernie took off his coroner's jacket and threw it over his shoulder. "I don't know why I brought this," he muttered. It had struck me from the beginning that his bringing the coat was about as sensible as a woman wearing high heels on the trail, but I said nothing. We all have our little vanities, and I remembered too clearly Annie's mirth at the sight of my African safari outfit and Tilley hat.

In the hopes that the topic would distract us both from the heat I asked, "Does the escort agency provide your full income, Ernie?"

"God, no," said Ernie, and he fished his wallet out of the back pocket of his jeans, flipped it open, took out a card, and handed it to me. I read,

Ernie Gold Personal Services Private Airport Limo Service. Property Management. Discreet Chauffeuring—Evening Hours. Boudoir & Aerial Photography. Memorabilia Collector (American Civil War). Waste Disposal Consulting. Expert Bra Fitting. Fruit Tree Spraying. Pest Exterminator. Fire-arms cleaned and oiled. Host of Lingerie Parties (Women Only). Fully Bonded.

"This is quite a business card, Ernie," I said. "Are you really bonded?"

"No," said Ernie. "But it makes people feel more confident if they read that you are. I'm all about making people feel confident."

"Tell me about the private limo service to the airport," I said.

Ernie cocked his head at me. "That one's not really legal," he said. "People take that one much more seriously than the escort agency stuff because there are licenses involved. I just rent myself out to people who want to be driven to the airport. Pick them up at their front door and deliver them to Toronto airport, and make arrangements to meet their plane when they get back. Simple as that. That way they don't have to worry about parking—and they sometimes hire me to keep an eye on the house while they're gone."

"Hence the *property management*," I said.

"Exactly," said Ernie. "But I don't really do that. I subcontract that out."

"Who to?" I asked.

"There's a biker gang in town," said Ernie, "and they're getting into some security businesses, but they need to use non-gang members to swing the contracts. I'm just the middleman. They check the places once a day—pick up the papers, collect the mail, water the flowers—and everyone's happy."

"And do your clients have any idea?" I asked, aghast at the thought of biker gangs operating security services.

"No, they don't know," said Ernie, "but they're happy because no one ever breaks in while they're gone. It works for everyone."

We had just rounded a bend in the trail, and on the right we both sighted, at the same moment, a small red house with a sign saying DOMM. This was certainly the home of the shrine we were looking for. It occurred to me in that moment, and I make the suggestion without charge to the Rotary Trail people, that it might be a good idea to identify home altars with a special, uniform sign of some kind—perhaps a black cross on a yellow background, or a red A on a green background. That way even people without the *Guide*—and they seem to be in the majority—will know where they are invited to stop. Anyway, the back yard of the little red house fronted right on the trail without a fence or even shrubs to define a boundary, so Ernie and I crossed the rather sad-looking lawn, climbed three rickety wooden stairs (more obstacles for the poor fellow in the wheelchair!), and knocked vigorously on the old and fragile back door.

The door was opened almost immediately by a rather heavy white woman in her mid-forties. I was struck simultaneously by two things: first, that she had lovely eyes, and second, that her home absolutely stank of cat feces. That's a curious conjunction, certainly, but that's what we encountered.

"Welcome!" said the woman. "I'm Roxy. Have you come to see my shrine?"

"Yes, we have," I said. "Do we catch you at a good time?"

"I'm happy to be caught any time," she laughed. "Come in." We entered, and as our eyes adjusted to the somewhat dimmer light we realised we were in the living room already, and that the shrine or altar was immediately in front of us. It was, as billed, a writing desk decorated with porcelain and glass cats, and it was flanked by two striking cat posters. There were, additionally (and as promised), no fewer than five food dishes at the base of the desk, and two bowls filled with water. Without the posters and the crockery, it might easily have passed for the sort of thing you'd find in the home of an eccentric and cat-crazy maiden aunt, but these accoutrements raised it a level or two to something else—though to what, I'm not absolutely sure.

"Don't be afraid to get closer!" urged Roxy, and we both took a step or two further in—and then stopped abruptly. The problem was that there were several piles of cat scat on the living room rug. Ernie and I looked at the scat, then exchanged glances with one another.

"Lady," said Ernie. "You've got cat shit all over the rug."

"Oh, don't worry about that," said Roxy. "It's all natural. Just go around it."

What do you do in circumstances like this? What do you do when someone who seems perfectly pleasant and welcoming invites you into her home—and reveals herself perfectly oblivious of the fact that there are piles of shit all over the room in which she proposes to entertain you? Do you just ignore this state of affairs? Do you offer to help her clean up? Do you thank her for her hospitality, but take the first opportunity to high-tail it out of there? I took a couple more tentative steps into the room. Ernie, however, stepped back.

"I ain't going any further," he said. "I'm not getting shit all over my shoes."

Roxy frosted up immediately. "Fine," she said. "Perhaps you'd like to wait outside." She stepped behind him and reopened the back door.

Ernie needed no further invitation. He moved toward the door, stepped over the threshold, and let out a great gush of air—as though he'd been holding his breath all the while he was inside. "Jeez, it stinks in there!" he said. "You should probably leave the door open, lady." So, of course, Roxy slammed it shut.

"Your friend is very rude," she said, turning and smiling brightly at me.

"Well, yes, he tends to speak his mind," I said, struggling between a certain loyalty to Ernie, and the desire to placate a madwoman. "He's from Kitchener," I added, rather feebly.

"Let's have a good, close look together," Roxy said, and to my alarm she took me by the hand and led me to the shrine. There followed a difficult ten minutes or so during which she identified each porcelain or glass cat by name, and told me where she'd bought it, or who gave it to her, and what its significance was in the warp and woof of her life. "This is Agatha," she said, "and this is Bronwen Feather-Paws, and this is Trigonometry."

"Why Trigonometry?" I asked, feeling that I had to say something.

"Because he was given to me by a math teacher," she explained. "He killed himself, poor thing."

"That's terrible," I said, realising suddenly that this little glass figure had depths and dimensions I could not hope to understand.

"He had a small penis," said Roxy. "It gnawed away at him."

"Well, I imagine it would," I said, trying desperately to get rid of the image her words had inadvertently conjured up.

"Most of them have," she added reflectively. "Math teachers. I've done a survey."

Ten minutes having passed, I felt I could, reasonably, begin to move toward the door—through whose little glass window Ernie was now peering from time to time.

"Well, you have a fabulous collection," I said, hoping to wind things up in a civilised way.

But Roxy was having none of it. There are people in this world who cannot read conversation-enders, who either choose not to—or cannot—see that other people wish to move on. Every gambit I tried, every "Well, thank you so much" or "I've really enjoyed," was met with another anecdote, another hand on the arm, another conversational sally. At one point, as I tried desperately (but politely) to engineer my retreat, Roxy quite deliberately stepped between me and the door, completely blocking my way. There was nothing threatening about the gesture, and she continued to smile brightly at me while she talked, but there was no disguising the fact that she was determined to have me stay and listen to her.

Suddenly, the back door opened, and there, like a deranged hillbilly, was Ernie, his hair all but standing on end, his eyes wild. "Lady, lady! It's terrible!" he shouted. "There's a big black dog in your front yard, and he's got this sweet little kitten in his mouth and he's shaking it!" Roxy screamed, clapped a hand to her mouth, and took off down the hall faster than a person her size should have been capable of moving. I was about to follow her, intending in some vague way to assist in rescuing this poor kitten, when Ernie grabbed me by the scruff of the neck and hauled me towards the back door. "Let's get out of here!" he shouted.

"But Ernie—the kitten!" I protested, as we tumbled down the back steps and hastened back towards the trail. Ernie let go of me, brushed his hair down, and looked me pityingly in the eyes.

"There isn't any kitten," he said.

"And the big black dog?" I said, ever slow on the uptake.

"There isn't any big black dog," Ernie said.

It took a moment or two to sink in. "Oh," I said. And then, a moment or two later, "Thank you."

"You're welcome," said Ernie, and we walked on together, I just beginning to register that my red-necked friend had effectively rescued me twice in the last forty minutes. But I was also remembering how lovely Roxy's eyes were, and wondering when the beautiful woman she must once have been was so overwhelmed by loneliness that she lost all good sense.

I'll close this chapter with one further piece of evidence that I'm often not the sharpest knife in the drawer. Some years back, and shortly after my first marriage ended, I lived with my two daughters in a tiny, two-bedroom apartment in Toronto. It was very much a temporary expedient, a transitional place, but it had to serve for about eight months. The bathroom was so small and had so little cupboard space that many of our medications and toiletries had to be left out in the open.

My older daughter and I both tend to develop mild acne when we're under stress, and this was certainly a stressful time. I was pleased, then, when I discovered she'd left her new face medication right next to the sink, which was in any event cheek by jowl with the toilet. So for the space of about a week I applied the cream to my complexion every morning after I'd shaved, and every night before I hopped into bed.

LOUISE

VISITING A FORMER GIRLFRIEND CAN BE A CHARGED BUSINESS. There's always the possibility that you have to meet the new boyfriend, in which case you spend the visit doing your best to reassure the new fellow, subtextually, that the old relationship is well and truly over, and you don't represent a threat at all. Absent that challenge there's the risk that an old flame might misinterpret the visit as a bid to start things up again, and respond unexpectedly. Generally speaking, however, my own visits with former girlfriends have gone reasonably well, and I'm very grateful for that because I like all of them (not that there's a great number), and am very glad that they're in the world doing what they do in precisely the way they do it.

Louise had sent me a map with an X marking where her house was on the trail, and I wasn't surprised to find that there was no room for confusion. She always was a careful and precise person, and it's remarkable she endured my own blundering imprecision for as long as she did. I had no idea what she'd make of Ernie, but I hoped that her natural hospitality would come to the fore.

What Ernie would make of *her* was another matter again: Louise was as reserved as Ernie was flamboyant, and I suspected and rather feared that Ernie might take delight in shocking her.

Louise's home was a pretty bungalow done up in blues and whites. It was separated from the trail by a low picket fence, surrounded by colourful flowerbeds, and reached by means of an unusual cobblestone path leading to the front door. "Of course Louise lives *there*," I thought when I saw it: the place reflected many of her own qualities—orderly, yes, but also attractive, welcoming and quietly elegant. She saw us coming up the path, and came out on her porch to greet us. I received a hug, which I thoroughly appreciated, coming as it did on the heels of my encounter with Roxy. Ernie got a pleasant handshake, and he seemed if anything a little cowed by Louise's slight formality. He was uncharacteristically quiet for the next little while, watching every move she made closely, and listening carefully to everything she said.

"Shall we have some iced tea on the porch?" Louise asked. "That way you can see some of the other pilgrims going by."

I looked at Ernie. "Whatever you suggest, ma'am," he said. So it was decided, and I brought a third chair round the house from the back yard, and we settled down, the three of us, to drink iced lemon tea and chat. And, not surprisingly, as time passed, Ernie loosened up a bit. "So you and Paul used to go out?" he said.

"Yes, we had a nice two years together," said Louise.

"What went wrong?" asked Ernie, cutting to the chase. I choked on my tea—and with every good intention Ernie thumped me vigorously on the back. Louise, however, remained perfectly calm and composed.

"Different priorities," she said sweetly.

"Yeah, it's often sexual," said Ernie, apparently tuned into a different conversation altogether. "Me and the old lady are pretty hit and miss these days."

"Really?" said Louise politely. Her eyes flicked to me just briefly, but they were disconcertingly eloquent.

"Yeah, it's all downhill once you hit forty," said Ernie. "Most of the guys I know have dinky-dos."

There was a pregnant silence. At last, Louise broke it. "What," she asked, "are dinky-dos?"

"That's when a guy's gut sticks out further than his dinky do," said Ernie, clearly surprised that anyone should be unfamiliar with this terminology. "Some guys have pretty big guts."

Louise sipped her tea reflectively. "What do you do for a living, Ernie?" she asked.

"I've got a little limo business," said Ernie expansively—and resolutely avoiding my eye. "Take people to the airport and pick them up again. And I do a little pest control on the side. If you've got rats or bats or termites, I'm the guy to call. No problem at all. Nice place you've got here."

"Thank you," said Louise. "I'm happy to say it's mostly pest-free."

Every now and then a little group of pilgrims passed by—sometimes in twos, sometimes in somewhat larger numbers. These, of course, would be people who had attended later blessings than we had, and set off later in the morning. I wondered how many had stopped by the Krupps and poor Roxy's. "Look," said Ernie, "there's the guy in the wheelchair."

And so it was. He was moving slowly now, clearly feeling the heat. "Is he a friend of yours?" asked Louise. "Would you like to offer him a glass of tea?"

Ernie rose to his feet. "Hey, wheelchair-guy!" he shouted. "Would you like a drink?" The gentleman in the wheelchair ignored him. He began moving faster along the trail, and in a moment or two disappeared behind some trees. "Well, that wasn't very polite," said Ernie, without a trace of irony.

We had a second glass of tea, and Louise told us a little about her work. She's a dietitian, and spends much of her time talking to community groups. She also gives supermarket tours, in which she walks around a food store showing people how to understand labels and where to find better foods. "Do you get free samples?" Ernie asked.

"Not usually," Louise told him. And then, seeing the question had not come out of nowhere, "May I offer you a sandwich and some cookies?" Ernie's eyes lit up. So Louise made us some sandwiches and brought out a plate of home-made oatmeal cookies, and we stayed, I fear, a little longer than we should have, though I think Louise enjoyed our company. She studied anthropology for her first degree, and having us visit must have seemed like relatively easy field research—the savages having come to her.

Just as we were stirring to leave, the front door opened and out came Louise's daughter, Kim—and I embarrassed myself by getting a little misty-eyed. Kim had been at least five years younger when last I'd seen her, and in the intervening years she'd changed from cute little girl into beautiful young woman. We greeted each other warmly, and I introduced her to Ernie. But even while we were all chatting I found myself thinking about my own children, and the children of my girlfriends and of other friends who have experienced divorce. So many of them seem so poised and worldly, but so many of them too have had difficulties of one kind or another—separation anxiety, night terrors, learning issues, free-floating anxiety, depression and chronic fatigue syndrome. I honestly don't know whether they would have had the same difficulties if their parents' various marriages had remained intact, but there are some studies, I know, that suggest otherwise, and I find Judith Wallerstein's work in this area particularly sobering and compelling. Most of the parents I know have bounced back from their divorces, but I worry about the kids, and I'm disproportionately grateful when I come across one who, like Kim, seems so comfortable, self-assured and happy. Louise had clearly done something right.

When we were taking our leave from Louise and Kim, Ernie surprised us with a very gallant gesture. Louise offered him her small hand to shake, but he took it in his big paw and bent to kiss it instead. The effect was a little spoiled by the fact that he smacked his lips loudly when he made contact, but his sincerity could not be doubted. Moments before this I'd asked whether

Louise might have a bottled water or two, and Ernie was now admirably set up. Louise had also offered to look after his jacket, and he had given it to her with marked relief. He was noticeably thoughtful as we moved on, and didn't say anything for a few minutes. "She's a good lady, Mason," he said at last.

"She is," I agreed.

"Pity you couldn't hold onto her," he added.

"I've got myself a good one," I said. And I have.

"You must have looked like Mutt and Jeff, though," he added. (Louise is tall; I'm not.)

I did not deign to reply.

But Ernie was really quite stuck on Louise. "Man," he said, "if she were a hooker, she'd be a Madam—and she'd run one classy whorehouse."

"You should have told her so," I suggested.

"No way, José!" said Ernie. "You don't talk to women like *that*." And he cast me a glance of such surpassing slyness that I knew he knew he had one-upped me very neatly.

We fell into a reasonably companionable silence for the next fifteen minutes or so. There was certainly plenty to see, and we took a voyeuristic pleasure in looking into people's front and back yards. If I were a natural storyteller I'd be able to fabricate some wonderful tales based simply on some of the tableaux we saw on back porches and front verandas. (As I'm not, however, and know it, I must stick to the truth.) By unspoken consent we passed by several home shrines with one-star ratings. I was disposed to think that the *Guide* writers knew exactly what they were doing in the matter of recommendations, and Ernie was full of sandwiches and oatmeal cookies and iced tea, to say nothing of two bowls of mega-meat soup and whatever he'd had for breakfast.

The back of a school eventually hove into view on the right side, and, rather to our surprise, its being Saturday, there were teenagers in the grounds playing Frisbee and talking. A knot of young men was moving across the lawn towards the trail, and they reached it just as we drew near. They were clad in baseball caps of varying hues, overlong T-shirts with the names of NBA teams stencilled on the front, and jean shorts whose crotches hung almost to their knees. Two of the five were also wearing wide leather bracelets with studs, and one of them had a goatish devil's head tattooed on his forearm.

One of them said, "Party at Sarah's tonight, eh?"

"Yeah. Got your two-four?" said another.

"Nah, I gotta bottle of rye. And some weed."

"I hear her parents are out of town," contributed another.

"It's gonna be a fucken mad house," said the first.

I nodded at them as we passed by, but they looked at me vacantly, almost as though I weren't there. I scarcely even registered on their radar.

Friends who teach high school tell me that it's the boys they worry about the most: so many of them have behavioural problems or are low achievers. Whenever I go to fast food restaurants I'm struck by the fact that for every young man behind the counter, there are five young women—and young women also vastly outnumber young men as clerks in the retail outlets I visit and, increasingly, on the grounds crews I see. My daughters and their female friends all have jobs—they're selling clothes, waiting tables, working cash registers, guiding tours, cutting lawns, testing water samples, guarding swimmers and selling movie tickets. They're also going off to university and community college in greater numbers than their male peers, and have already become a majority presence in many professional programs. As the father of daughters, and as a man who loves women, I celebrate every advance that women make. But I worry about the boys, and wonder why political rhetoric still focuses on the need to empower girls and win equality for them, when it's demonstrably the boys who are in greater need of help. My friends in the baseball caps looked and sounded as dumb as the proverbial sack full of hammers, but unless we reach them somehow—unless we find ways to excite them about learning and

achievement—we're going to be dealing with them in unemployment lines, the courts and fringe political parties in the years
to come. And yes, I know there are exceptions—wonderful, shining examples of male success—but they are, by definition, exceptions. We have a problem.

I asked Ernie, "What did you think of those lads?"

He shrugged. "Just your typical white trash," he answered.

"What would you do with them?" I persisted.

"Put 'em in the army," said Ernie. We soldiered on.

We had just passed a row of nicely sited town homes, when we
saw, by the side of the trail, a young man sitting on a chair behind
a table covered with plastic cups. Underneath the table was a large
cooler, and we quickly realised we'd happened upon a trail-side
lemonade stand. "You thirsty, Ernie?" I asked, mostly joking.

"Depends how much he's charging," said Ernie seriously. And
then, "He's a coloured boy." I winced.

If the young fellow heard, and he probably had, he showed no
sign of it. "Good morning, gentlemen," he sang out cheerfully. As
we got closer I saw that he was probably older than I had first
thought—sixteen, perhaps, rather than twelve or thirteen. And he
was a stunningly friendly and presentable young man, quite unlike
the boys we'd just passed. I'd guess, too, that he was Arabic,
though he was dressed in a Western-style shirt and pair of shorts.

"Good morning," I said. "You're an enterprising fellow to be
out on the trail like this."

"Lots of business here," he said happily. "It's a hot day and
people get thirsty."

"How much?" said Ernie, a bit brusquely.

"There's no charge," said the young man.

"No charge?" I said.

"What's the catch?" asked Ernie suspiciously.

"No catch," said the young man. "This is my gift." He opened
the cooler, lifted out a glass jug, and filled two plastic cups.
"Please," he said. "Take. Drink." We took, and we drank. And it

was delicious lemonade. We saw, moreover, that there was a receptacle for the dirty cups, suggesting that the young man intended carting them away.

"Okay," said Ernie. "Do we have to listen to some sort of sales pitch now?"

"No," said the young man. "You're free to go. Have a wonderful day. Are you on the pilgrimage?"

"Yes," I said. "We're going through to Lakefield."

"Then I'd ask you to do one thing, if you wouldn't mind," he said.

"Hah!" said Ernie triumphantly, his suspicions confirmed.

"What's that?" I asked.

"Say a prayer for me when you get to the church," he said.

Ernie and I paused for a moment, wondering if the young man was having us on. But he wasn't. "What's your name?" I asked.

"Ali," he said. "Ali Manji."

"Ali," said Ernie, testing the name on his tongue. "Are you a Christian?"

"No, I'm a Muslim," said Ali.

"And you want us to say a prayer for you in a Christian church?" said Ernie.

"The same God hears our prayers, wherever we pray from," said Ali, smiling. I could see that Ernie was wrestling with images of jet planes flying into skyscrapers, and thousands of Arabs shaking their fists in the air and shouting, "Death to the Great Satan!"—but the evident goodness of the young man in front of us won out.

"I will, then," said Ernie gruffly.

"I will, too," I said.

"Thank you," he said, and he extended his hand. We shook hands with him, put our cups into the receptacle, and moved on again. But we took away more than slaked thirsts and the taste of fresh lemonade. We also took away a sense of how things might be if we all truly believed and lived out the precepts of our various faiths.

ROSEMARY

NOT ALL THE TRAFFIC WAS HEADED TOWARDS LAKEFIELD. SOME people, the bulk of whom were probably local Peterborough folk, were just out for a walk and moving against the tide. If they were frustrated at encountering so much traffic coming the other way they gave no sign of it. (And not all the people going towards Lakefield were pilgrims, either. Some of them, too, were locals just stretching their legs.) In the first few minutes after we parted from Ali Manji we encountered, at brief intervals, a bikini-clad girl and a muscle-shirted young man on roller blades, two mothers pushing strollers, and a dad and his two young daughters, all three on bikes. The mothers and the dad smiled at us, but Ms Bikini and Mr Muscle Shirt were very much wrapped up in each other, and not disposed to notice anyone who wasn't equally flat-bellied, chisel-featured, windswept and radiating killer hormones.

Every now and then we caught a glimpse of the Otonabee River. Usually it was just a patch of blue seen through trees, but here and there along the trail we had an uninterrupted view, and when this happened we were mildly surprised at the number of boats we saw. Some of these were houseboats; others were cruisers of one kind or another. A lot of wealthy people go through these locks, working their way from some of the northern lakes down through Peterborough to Rice Lake, and from there, if they're so minded, further south still to Lake Ontario.

Roughly ten minutes after we parted from Ali we came to a home that looked like nothing so much as an English cottage, and I knew, both from the *Guide* and from the WELCOME PILGRIMS sign, that this was one of the most highly rated home shrines on the route. It belonged, it appeared, to another single lady—which briefly gave me pause—but we were both encouraged by the five-star rating, and by this comment in the *Guide*:

> The shrine has been built outside, but is viewed through the window of a comfortable sitting room. Rosemary Venables has requested that we not describe the shrine in this publication, but we will attest that it is eminently worth the visit.

After reading this aloud to Ernie I said, "That sounds promising." He nodded thoughtfully, and I took his silence to signal consent. We opened an old-fashioned garden gate in a low hedge, made our way up the path, and rang Ms Venables' doorbell.

I will confess that my heart sank a little when Rosemary opened the door, because she was, like Roxy, a fairly large lady, but the resemblance was superficial. While Roxy's energy was focused in a way that was, ultimately, needy and depressing, Rosemary was colourful but also centred. She greeted us, and greeted us warmly, but she didn't *attach* herself to either of us. She was clearly glad to meet us, but she didn't *need* to meet us.

"I'm so glad you've come," she said, smiling and opening the door wide for us to enter.

"Should we take our shoes off?" I asked. Her floors were polished hard wood, with colourful rugs that looked vaguely Turkish.

"That would be very kind," she answered. "Just put them on that mat." The mat was clearly designed to accommodate many pairs of shoes, and I marvelled at our good fortune in arriving at a time when other people were not also there. We followed Rosemary down her hallway, then turned left into what I at first took to be a study, but quickly learned was at once a consulting room and a kind of viewing station. Three chairs, fortuitously, were grouped together in the centre of the room, and all looked out a large, glass sliding door—a door that took up practically the whole wall—overlooking the most beautiful pocket garden I have ever seen.

What do I mean by *pocket garden*? I mean a garden that could not have been much larger than twenty feet wide by thirty feet deep. In the foreground was a gorgeous pond that seemed to come right up to the edge of the house: if I'd stepped out the door I would have been knee-deep in sun-dappled water. And in the background, and curving around on both sides of the house, were ascending terraces of earth and rock and shrubs. A small waterfall drew one's attention to the centre of the scene. It was, then, a Japanese-style garden, but there were subtle subversions of that aesthetic here and there—a little too much colour in the flora, principally (Japanese gardens traditionally use a limited palette)—and a stone statue of a man carrying a laughing child on his back across the pond.

"Saint Christopher?" I asked.

"Yes, Saint Christopher," said Rosemary. "Please, have a seat. Make yourselves comfortable." So we sat down.

My mind is not easily quieted. I spend much of my time worrying about one thing or another, and more time than seems altogether healthy entertaining sexual fantasies. More constructively, perhaps, I will sometimes use restful moments to try to think through problems—how I might cheer up one of my children; when it would be convenient to take the car in for servicing; what Mr Bush should do in Iraq; whether to buy Annie a table-saw or an evening gown for her birthday; why the apple tree in my garden is sick. I'm pretty good at looking calm and at ease, but the truth is that I rarely am. In Rosemary's consulting room, however, I quickly felt balanced, centred, at peace.

Ernie asked, "Why do you call this a consulting room?"

"I'm a prayer counsellor," said Rosemary, "and this is where I work with the people who come to see me."

"What does a prayer counsellor do?" I asked.

"People have problems," said Rosemary. "Perhaps it's a sick parent, or a child who's not doing well. Perhaps their marriage is in trouble. Maybe they're facing sickness themselves. They come to see me, and we talk about their problem, and then we pray together. In this room."

"Then you're a kind of therapist," I said.

"I suppose I am," said Rosemary, "but I'm a great deal cheaper." She laughed. "And I don't have any qualifications, except that I listen well and care about the people who come to see me."

"How much do you cost?" asked Ernie, putting the question that was on my own mind, but which I'd felt it indelicate to float.

"Twenty dollars an hour," said Rosemary. "If the person can afford it."

"And what if he can't?" asked Ernie.

"Then it's cheaper—or it's free," said Rosemary. "My home is paid for, so I don't need much income."

The only time I'd previously heard the words *prayer counsellor* was on a televangelist show where the host was exhorting viewers to call his panel of prayer counsellors. My sense then, rightly or wrongly, was that this was a fund-raising ploy, and that using a prayer counsellor would inevitably lead to a request for a *love offering* of $250. What to make of this, then? Was this lady a charlatan or a woman who, for modest recompense, lightened people's loads a little? I'm still not entirely sure, but I can affirm that simply sitting with her in that room made me feel quietly happy. Of course, it may have been largely the extraordinary scene outside the window combined with the comfort of my chair—but she was the lady, after all, who had designed the garden and set up the room, so whether her influence was direct or indirect it was still palpable and benevolent.

"Did you build the shrine for your counselling, or for the pilgrimage?" I asked.

"I'd created the garden before I decided to set up as a prayer counsellor," Rosemary replied. "But when I did set up, I knew that this was the room where I wanted to see people. And when the pilgrimage began, and someone suggested that residents on the trail might open their homes to people making the walk, it just seemed to make sense to join in."

"What do you think of the whole pilgrimage thing?" asked Ernie.

"I think it's quite wonderful," Rosemary said. "I only knew Daz by sight, but she was clearly a lovely lady. And if people are being healed when they come into the presence of the statue she made, that's a gift, isn't it? And meanwhile people like me have the chance to open their homes to other people, and share what they've created. I see the whole pilgrimage route as God's necklace, and these little shrines along the way are like the beads. So this shrine is a bead on God's necklace."

So we sat and looked at the garden for about ten minutes, largely without speaking, and that was not something I'd ever have predicted or expected. We're not, Ernie and I, the sort of fellows who normally gaze at anything *still*—not the sort of men you'd find traipsing around art galleries, for example. But we gazed, and we thought—or, I should say, *I* thought, because I cannot with certainty describe Ernie's thoughts—peaceful thoughts.

"May I offer you some tea?" Rosemary asked at length, and she rose to make it.

"No—no, thank you," I answered quickly, even at the risk of raising Ernie's ire. "You've given us something precious," I said, and I meant it. It didn't seem right somehow to muddy the visit with food or drink.

We did visit the bathroom, however, and this small courtesy touched me. How many people would feel comfortable letting perfect strangers use their most intimate facilities? The trail currently has very, very few public washrooms, and the generosity of people like Rosemary is really pretty formidable.

Just as we were walking up the hall the doorbell rang, so our parting from Rosemary was complicated by her need to welcome her new guests—three spry old ladies in tracksuits and expensive walking shoes. I did see a tiny box marked DONATIONS by the door, however, and needed no prompting to slip a bill through the slot. Rosemary's home may be paid for, but I'd guess she's not a wealthy woman—not if her only source of income is the occasional $20—and what she's done and what she's doing deserve recompense. Ernie followed suit, and if you take the pilgrimage yourself I'd encourage you to give some token to those who make you richly welcome.

Both the *Guide* and the glossy pamphlet from the Tourism Bureau showed that we were now drawing even with the Riverside Zoo on the opposite side of the Otonabee. The zoo was there during my student days at Trent, but the map shows its attached parklands have been significantly added to in recent years. (After I'd finished the pilgrimage I took a walk through the area, and was hugely impressed with what I saw, and amazed at how few people I encountered. This is surely one of Peterborough's jewels, and well worth a visit even if you're not interested in the animals.) The thickness of the brush on our left at this point of the trail meant that we could not see the zoo, but knowing it was there reminded me of an evening in 1978 when I inadvertently made a complete ass of myself.

In the spring of my third year at Trent, the university's theatre society produced one of my plays. The play's closing coincided with the end of classes, so it seemed a good excuse to throw a party. My then-girlfriend, Kathy, and I supplied a huge batch of lasagne and some beer, but there was an unspoken understanding that guests would also contribute something, and our guests were generous. Someone brought a tossed salad, someone else a cheesecake, and there were all sorts of snacking foods of one kind or another on the table. One young lady, whom I did not know very well, brought some very impressive-looking brownies. I'm a sucker for chocolate, and I like brownies. I mean I like brownies a *great* deal. I had one, then I had another, and other people didn't seem to like them as much as I did, so I had another, and the young lady who'd made them encouraged me to have still another—so, to be polite, I did.

Things had been going smoothly; this was a pleasant gathering, and I was having fun. I had been sitting down to eat my final brownie, and to chat with the lady who'd cooked them (who was watching me with great interest), when I heard a loud noise in the next room. I rose to go and see what was happening, and promptly discovered something surprising: someone had moved the kitchen door. In fact, not content with moving the door, they'd moved the whole wall and switched around a couple of the others. Additionally—and you can imagine my befuddlement—my feet seemed an astonishing distance from my head, and when I bent down to make sure they were still there, I realised that the texture and colours of the kitchen rug were more fascinating than I had ever dreamed, and that there were tiny little crocodiles—friendly crocodiles, fortunately—waltzing all over the floor.

"Paul, what are you doing?" asked Kathy, when she came in to find me on my hands and knees, trying to catch the little baby crocodiles that were now playing hide and seek all around me.

"Your boyfriend has just eaten more Jamaican grass than anyone on the face of the earth has ever eaten before," said our guest. The rest of the evening is a bit of a blur, but I have a hazy memory of someone driving a group of us to the zoo to set off some fireworks. And when the police arrived there, a few minutes later, I'm told that I was busy trying to persuade my crocodiles (who had come along for the ride) to vote for the New Democratic Party.

I was remembering these events, and brooding over the fact that the brownie-chef is now regularly interviewed on the CBC on matters unrelated to her culinary expertise, when we reached a little pedestrian bridge over a stream leading to the river. Four children of about five through seven—two girls and two boys—were leaning over the railing and dropping leaves and twigs into the water. A woman I took to be their mother was hovering over them watchfully, but clearly enjoying their enjoyment. "Good morning," I said (for it was still morning, if only just).

"Good morning," she said. Ernie and I stopped and watched the children playing for a moment.

"Which ones are yours?" Ernie asked companionably.

"Oh, all of them," said the woman. She was a sturdy-looking lady in her late thirties, plainly but nicely dressed. The children all wore shorts, T-shirts and sun hats, and I was close enough to see that their skin shone in the way it does when sun-screen has been recently applied.

"All of them!" said Ernie. "They must keep you busy."

I smiled fondly. It was somehow pleasant to see my friend Ernie interacting in a family-man sort of way with this nice mother.

"They do," said the lady. "But these are only some of them."

"How many do you have?" I asked.

"Eleven," said the lady. "Eleven little soldiers for Christ."

I was taken aback. Ernie was thunderstruck, but rallied quickly to make what I thought was rather a good joke. "Jesus, lady," he said, "pop just one more and you'd have your own band of disciples!"

The children turned from their game and looked solemnly at the two of us. "There's no need for profanity," said the older of the two girls.

"Number twelve is on the way," said the mother, patting her belly gently. And then, fixing us with a bright eye: "Christians need to have more children. There's a terrible battle coming."

"A battle with whom?" I asked. But she didn't answer me.

"Come along, children. Grandpa will be wondering where we are," she said. The little party promptly moved off in the direction from which we'd just come, the boys taking the lead, and the girls falling in behind their mother. Ernie and I watched them go in silence.

MRS X

TWELVE NOON FOUND US CROSSING ARMOUR ROAD, AND HEADING into the last leg of the trail before we would see Trent. I was looking forward to seeing my old university. Though I am, my wife and daughters tell me, breathtakingly sentimental, I am not terribly sentimental about Trent: a few years on various university committees cured me of any naiveté. But I met some good people there, and learned some good things, and did some growing up, and I certainly have fond memories of the campus, with its drumlins and wildlife sanctuary, and the river flowing right through the heart of it. If your children are contemplating university, or if you're of that age yourself, it's worth checking out—particularly if you're a left-wing, dope-smoking, anti-American bisexual deconstructionist.

We had just crossed the road and were mopping our brows and wondering (in my case) if I dared take my shirt off once we reached the wilder reaches of the trail, when we almost ran into a couple of blond-haired young men advancing from the north. They were moving with such speed, arms pumping away, that they'd simply have rolled over anyone smaller than Ernie and me. "I'm sorry," I said, in the idiotic way some of us have of apologising when we ourselves have been wronged. What I actually meant, of course, was, "Watch where you're going, you mindless gits."

But they weren't mindless gits: they were Germans.

I confess I have a conflicted relationship with Germans. Most of my older relatives are English and Scots, and they tell heartrending stories of having to take refuge in bomb shelters and the Tube while the *Luftwaffe* dropped a range of fiendishly inventive munitions on London, Canterbury and Bristol—to say nothing of poor Coventry. There's a lot of residual anger there, in spite of the fact that my aging ancestors are not Jewish and the *Volk* weren't actually trying to wipe us out. But there surely comes a point where one has to let go of that anger (I'm speaking for the Mason/Nash clan here—I wouldn't presume to speak for the Jews), recognising that pretty well every race on the planet has behaved abysmally at some point or another. And no, I certainly don't exempt my own people.

Complicating my relationship with Germans is the fact that I keep bumping into nice ones—warm, generous, cultured, hardworking folk. It's a bit disconcerting when people refuse to live up to their national stereotype.

"So you're Krauts, are you?" said Ernie, when he realised that Chris and Martin's home town, Munich, is in Germany.

"Ernie!" I remonstrated with him. "They're *Germans*! Not *Krauts*. They're our friends and allies. We're in NATO together."

"Oh," said Ernie, apparently not fully convinced.

Our two hikers occupied a sort of No Man's Land between Civilised World Citizen and Teutonic Stereotype. They were certainly fine specimens physically, but there was something off-putting about the fact they didn't quite look at us when they spoke—though, admittedly, Ernie and I were far from being fine specimens physically ourselves, and were probably not very nice to look at. We're not the sort of men that people are going to photograph and post up on their walls, except perhaps as models of male-pattern baldness and the dangers of spreading girths.

"You are going to Lakefield, yah?" said Martin.

"Is it still there?" asked Ernie, managing to imply that if it weren't, Chris and Martin were probably responsible somehow.

Fortunately, Martin and Chris missed the implication. "Dull little village. Not vorth fisiting," said Chris.

"Were you there yesterday?" I asked.

"This morning," said Martin, showing off a splendid set of teeth. "Ve rose at five and ran there before breakfast, and ve looked around, and now ve are speed-valking back to Peterborough for lunch."

This struck me as a bit show-offy. It's one thing to be an athletic superman, but quite another to make everyone else feel hopelessly inadequate.

"It's weird we missed seeing you," said Ernie.

Chris and Martin looked at him with some surprise. *I* looked at him with bewilderment.

"This is our third round-trip today," said Ernie. "And we got started late."

"Ve didn't see you on the trail," said Martin, his eyes narrowing, and his moustache making a little implication of its own.

"That's because we went by river the first two times," said Ernie, and he made a swinging motion with his arms that was probably meant to suggest the Australian front crawl: the two Germans stepped back in some alarm. "Got to keep to schedule, guys," said Ernie, and with that he took my arm firmly and moved me on down the trail toward Trent, leaving Chris and Martin to march into Peterborough and plot the invasion of Campbellford at their own pace.

Not four minutes later, and just as I was composing a little speech about racial tolerance and the marvels of multiculturalism, I was suddenly hailed by the male half of a middle-aged couple approaching us, again, from the opposite direction. "Paul Mason!" he cried. "What the hell are *you* doing here?"

The questioner was a heavyset, bearded fellow, and it frankly took me a second or two to remove his beard (in my mind's eye) and recognise him as an old friend from Lady Eaton College at Trent. "Bernie!" I cried. "God, it's been twenty years!" Occasions like this don't find me at my most articulate. I'm afraid I'm fast becoming the sort of avuncular fellow who's forever saying things like, "My, how you've grown!" and "I remember when you were potty-trained!" to the eye-rolling ennui of my friends' children, and the intense embarrassment of my own.

So we shook hands warmly, and he introduced his wife Cheryl, and I introduced Ernie, and Bernie and Cheryl explained that they had brought their second child to see Trent, so that he could decide whether he wanted to apply in the fall. He was currently receiving a tour of the prime orgy and demonstration spots, and Bernie and Cheryl had seized the opportunity to check out the Rotary Greenway trail, about which they'd heard from friends in the Peterborough area.

I'd always liked Bernie. He was a friendly, easy-going fellow, who embraced life warmly and laughed in great gusts. It pleased me that he'd married and had children, and that they were now venturing out into the wider world. It also saddened me, a little, that we hadn't stayed in touch.

I asked, "What's your son interested in studying?"

"Geography," said Bernie "—just like his old man. But who knows? He may change his mind once he gets here."

"Why are you here?" asked Cheryl, and so I explained. "What an interesting thing to do," she said. "If we weren't going to Kingston tomorrow, I'd want to come along, too."

And so our conversation proceeded—with a pleasant sharing of information, an expression of good wishes, and an exchange of email addresses. Typical, unremarkable, and perhaps scarcely worth mentioning, except that Bernie called to my memory someone as our conversation was drawing to an end. "Do you remember Mrs X?" he asked.

I did remember Mrs X—and I don't use her real name only in deference to her family's express wish. Bernie and I had met Mrs X in 1977, when she would have been in her mid-forties. She was the wife of a gentleman who commuted to Scarborough every day, and there made enough money that she could remain at home and focus on raising their children. Mrs x was a devoted mother and wife: she was also Jewish—though she was, I think, a liberal and mostly secular Jew. Mr x, for his part, was a devoted father and husband: he was, moreover, a Sikh, though far from being strict in his observances. I suspect (though I don't know this for sure) that they had each decided to make little of their religious heritages so that neither felt excluded from that part of the other's life.

Anyway, on a Thanksgiving weekend in the early 1970s Mrs x had gone for a walk on the Trent campus, and was struck by the fact that she ran into a number of solitary students who clearly had not been able to return to their homes on this holiday. This seemed sad to her. She knew someone at Trent, and through her she was able, informally, to find the names of some of these young people, and she invited them to her home for a Thanksgiving meal. And so began a tradition that lasted twenty-seven years.

Who was welcome? Anyone—and up to six at a time. There were kids from Ethiopia, and from Windsor; from Thailand and from Sudbury; from West Timor and from the Eastern Townships of Quebec. Her husband would pick them up at a designated spot and ferry them back home. They would be fed soup and rolls, roast turkey and cranberry sauce, potatoes and squash, pumpkin pie and ice cream, and they'd drink juice and finish with tea or coffee. There was never alcohol, but there was plenty of everything else.

What there was plenty of was, mostly, grace—and when I say *grace*, I mean unearned generosity and kindness. People would sit down at her table strangers—to their hosts and, as often as not, to each other—and would rise friends. We came with our hunger and our loneliness, and we were fed: we got turkey, and we got fellowship.

I attended only one of those meals: the following year found me entrenched in a network of friends and family. Some people, however (including Bernie), were repeat guests through their undergraduate years. Mrs X liked to stay in touch. You were likely to receive a call or a note a few weeks after the meal. Were you worried about exams? Were you going home for Christmas? Had things worked out with the new girlfriend?

Inevitably, I suppose, there was sometimes friction between guests: the year after the first Gulf War brought a young man from Tel Aviv and a young man from Baghdad to the table. They began the meal with barbed words and hostile glares: they ended the evening with a handshake. At that charged time, that one small act was in itself a kind of miracle.

But the greater miracle was, surely, that Mrs X kept up this loving tradition, fully supported by her husband, for those many years. For twenty-seven years she added a leaf to the dining room table, set an extra five or six placemats, cooked an extra large turkey, and fed it to people who, at first, she knew only as names. Let's say that, conservatively speaking, she gave a dinner they'll remember for the rest of their lives to at least a hundred different young people. Who knows what loneliness she alleviated? Who knows what friendships she made possible? Who knows what kindnesses some of her guests have been moved to do themselves in the years since? Grace is contagious.

Trent came into sight about ten minutes later, though we'd stopped once or twice, briefly, to admire a tiny little red bird flying and singing amid the tree branches close to the trail. At this stage in the journey, however, we had to take to the road for about a half kilometre before we could get back on the trail. This is far from being a tragedy, but it's a bit of a shame, and I hope that Trent eventually finds a way to allow the trail to run through its own land holdings. We walked along the right-hand side of Nassau Mills Road, crossing a bridge over the Trent canal and rounding a fairly long bend before we could see the university again. At this stage, however, we had a clear and uninterrupted view of both the river and the main structures of the school, including the pedestrian bridge.

Seeing the Athletic Complex, the Bata Library (where I spent too little time), the bridge, Champlain College and the drumlin behind Lady Eaton College brought another surge of memories: I remembered meeting my first wife for the first time; I remembered arguing with a gifted professor and theatre director, now lost to AIDS; and I remembered too, with somewhat less enthusiasm, a rather pompous student union president (or chairperson, in Trent nomenclature) who saw his battles with the university administration as roughly analogous to Winston Churchill's war with Nazi Germany. I thought, "I wonder what he's doing now?" I'd heard that he'd become a junior civil servant, and I succumbed briefly to the unworthy hope that he was making a derisory wage, hemmed in by bureaucratic restraints, battling a cholesterol problem and brooding over numerous roads not taken. But that was me, you know: that was me. And people grow up, and move on, and maybe light a few candles here and there. I hope I have.

Gesturing toward a large building under construction on the east side of the river, Ernie asked, "What's that?"

The fact that I read my alumni magazine meant I had an answer. "That's one of the new colleges," I said. "I think that one's going to be named after Peter Gzowski."

"Gzowksi," said Ernie, frowning slightly. "*Peter* Gzowski. Isn't that the stuttering guy on CBC radio who thought all women were oppressed, and that men should be castrated, or something?"

"No, Ernie," I said crossly. "Peter Gzowski was a CBC radio host, but he was a very fair-minded man and his program was hugely popular."

"Sure, with privileged middle-class women who imagined they were oppressed," said Ernie darkly. "They tuned in to hear how rotten their lives were, then they ragged on their husbands when they got home from work."

I tried hard, for a moment or two, to get indignant about this

unkind characterisation of a Canadian icon, but I figured that
Mr Gzowski's shoulders were broad enough, even posthumously,
to shrug off Ernie's barbs. And, as with a number of Ernie's other
generalisations, it's possible there was a grain of truth in the criticism. In all the years I listened to Mr Gzowski—and I was a real
fan—I never once heard him challenge a feminist writer, a native
spokesman, or the representative of an aggrieved minority. And
while I tended to share much of his left-liberalism, I can see why
someone with a more conservative point of view might swiftly
come to feel sidelined and disenfranchised.

"I was sad when he died," I said. And I was. And I had plenty
of company.

We passed under the pedestrian bridge, and briefly crossed to
the other side of the road to look across the river at Trent's
Champlain College. It was designed by the fine Canadian archi-
tect Ron Thom, and it looks quite marvellous in the spring, summer and fall when the leaves are out. In the winter, however, it
looks rather like a medieval fortress, and its monochromatic grey
face tends to encourage bleak thoughts. On this occasion,
though, it was high summer, the sun was shining and it was hot,
and as we stood there a bare-chested young man in a pair of
shorts walked down the steps beside the river, paused a moment,
then plunged in. A moment later, two other people emerged
from one of Champlain's towers, stripped off their own tops, and
joined him in the water. As the latter two were both lithe young
women, Ernie and I continued watching with keen interest and
approval.

"This is your old school, eh?" said Ernie.

"Yes," I said, "I did my BA here."

"Did you have lots of girlfriends?" Ernie asked.

I briefly considered laying claim to great hordes of eager bed
mates, but after a moment's reflection realised there was no point
at all. "No," I answered truthfully.

"You sorry now?" asked Ernie.

"Sometimes I think I should have played the field a bit more," I said.

"I like cats," said Ernie, and for one bewildering moment I thought we'd slipped into some parallel universe, and that familiar words now stood for completely different things. I quickly realised, however, that Ernie had spied a cat making its way along the riverbank with an American goldfinch in its mouth. We watched it pass us, heading for a quiet place to tear apart its prey.

The first time that Annie and I spent the night together I took it upon myself to remove her large cat, Mr Smudge, from the bed and put him outside the door. He seemed surprised, but accepting, and slunk off somewhere. When we went downstairs the following morning, however, we found that he had sought out my shoes, positioned by the front door, and pooped generously in both of them. He had then, in a gesture of further feline defiance, dragged his bum along the hall's linoleum floor to create a pretty impressive skid mark. The message could not have been more eloquent. After a few weeks, happily, we found our way to a respectful accommodation: I fed him regularly, and scratched him under the chin and behind the ears, and he accepted the food and the scratching as his just right, dominion and due, and left my shoes alone.

"I'm a dog man myself," I said to Ernie.

But another synapse had fired in Ernie's brain, and he was now watching the topless swimmers cavorting happily in the waters of the Otonabee with, on his part, a mixture of lust and regret. "Maybe *I* should have gone to university," he said.

At length we turned away from the swimmers, re-crossed the road, and were confronted immediately with what I think is Trent's environmental science building—new since my time at Trent, but certainly not in the context of all the building that's currently underway. Before we'd gone underneath the bridge I'd wondered if the structure was meant to resemble the front end of a Canada goose. Now, from this rear view, I was struck by two features: something that looked rather like a nipple—but leave room here for some imaginative carry-over from the naked swimmers—and an odd sort of afterthoughty back-end thing that vaguely suggested an unfinished barn.

"What's that?" asked Ernie.

"The nipple or the barn?" I said.

"The barn," said Ernie.

"It's a post-modern semiotic allusion to the disappearance of the family farm," I said, taking a game stab at it. (I once took a course in cultural studies. And I got an A. On condition that I switch out of the program.)

"What's the good of a barn without walls?" asked Ernie.

"I don't know," I said honestly.

"It's not functional," Ernie observed. "It doesn't do anything."

"No," I agreed.

"And it's not beautiful," said Ernie.

"No," I said. And it certainly *isn't* beautiful.

Ernie thought about this for a moment. "A lot of university stuff is just bullshit, isn't it?" he said.

"Yes," I agreed again, and having thus blithely dismissed a millennium's worth of intellectual exploration and critical enquiry, we set our sights on the Lakefield leg of the pilgrimage trail.

DOUG AND THE VIRGIN MARY

THE TRAIL *between* PETERBOROUGH AND LAKEFIELD IS ALTOGETHER more rustic than the trail *within* Peterborough—though you can imagine yourself in the country even within Peterborough itself. On the Lakefield leg you can, at points, see the Otonabee River, and you probably see more of it along this stretch than while you're in Peterborough, if only because there are many fewer houses in the way. But there are some houses along the route— though they tend to come either singly or in small clumps—and a surprising number of these contain home shrines. The vegetation for much of the walk is pleasantly lush, even in a hot July, and features many trees. There's a lot of bird life.

There is one small settlement between Peterborough and Lakefield, but you have to take a branch of the trail to find it. The gorgeously named Hamlet of Frodo is a community of about forty houses, a tiny church and a general store. Ernie and I did visit it, but we'll come to that later. If I should live long enough to retire, that's where I'd like to make my home, and that's where I want to be buried.

We had not been back on the trail for more than five minutes when we came upon a very tall young man sitting on his backpack and drinking from a water bottle. I'd guess that he was about twenty-three, and we soon learned that he was between his honours year of a fine arts degree and the start of his B.Ed. in September. Doug appeared to think carefully before he spoke—a habit that came to irritate Ernie profoundly—but while I first thought this was because he wanted to weigh his words and judge their impact (an admirable thing!), I eventually concluded it was because he had to channel enormous effort into seeming even remotely normal. I'm not joking. I came to like the man very much in the brief time we were together, but I'm only giving his first name because he's probably teaching somewhere in Ontario and I think it's important that students be exposed to the odd harmless lunatic before the school board realises just who it's hired. But if your child tells you one day that his art class has spent the last three weeks in school bathrooms painting murals of the Virgin Mary on a white stallion, well, ask whether the teacher's name is Doug.

"Hallo," said Ernie. "Hot work, eh?"

"Yes . . . [Count eight!] It is hot," said Doug.

"Good thing you brought along some water," said Ernie.

". . . Yes," said Doug.

We had stopped, and pulled our own water bottles out of my knapsack to keep our new friend company. I asked, "When did you leave Daz's house?"

Doug thought long and hard about this one—so long and hard that Ernie tapped his forehead significantly. "Guy's a bit slow," he said.

". . . I left at 9.30," said Doug. ". . . And I'm *not* slow," he added.

"Well, Special Guy, it's been great chatting with you," said Ernie, "but we need to get going again." He took one final pull on his water bottle, then put the cap back on and began putting it back in my knapsack.

". . . Can I keep you company?" asked Doug.

Absolutely nothing in Ernie's demeanour could have signalled that this would be a welcome prospect, and I was astonished that Doug should *want* to join us. But we were all pilgrims after all, and Ernie seemed to feel compelled to welcome him—in his own Ernie-ish way. "Sure," said Ernie. "But speak faster, would ya?"

" . . . Okay," said Doug, trimming a good half second off his response time. Ernie rolled his eyes, and we set off together, and exchanged, during the next few minutes, such information as I've given you above—names, education, jobs and what have you.

"So you're going to be a teacher, eh?" said Ernie, his tone revealing that he saw most teachers as lazy, overpaid, under-worked rip-off artists who entered the profession largely because of the lengthy holidays, frequent professional development days, and annual opportunities to go on strike. (Trent graduates a lot of teachers.)

" . . . Yes," said Doug. "I want to mould young minds in the image of Christ."

"You want to do what?!" said Ernie.

" . . . Mould young minds—" began Doug.

"Yes, I heard you," said Ernie. "But I didn't think you were allowed to do that in public schools."

" . . . I'm going to teach in the *Catholic* system," said Doug.

"Oh, Jesus, he's a Catholic," said Ernie. Being a Catholic, I quickly gathered, was almost as bad as being a feminist or a communist.

" . . . Is there something wrong with being a Catholic?" asked Doug.

Ernie rolled his eyes again. "No, it's just wonderful," he said. "You stick with it. It'll save you from ever having to think for yourself. That's great. No problem at all."

We walked on in silence for some minutes, Ernie looking grim, Doug seeking guidance from above, and me wondering whether my first wife's Catholicism had ever prevented her from thinking for herself. It certainly had never prevented her from *disagreeing* with me—but it's at least remotely possible that some of our arguments flowed from the different ways we saw and understood the world, and that those differences were shaped (or at least influenced) by differences in our religious upbringing. Early training runs deep, and differences that seem trivial in the afterglow of a good lovemaking session can seem much larger a few years later on.

"My first wife was Catholic," I said aloud. "And so is Louise. And so is Annie, for that matter."

"Mixed marriages never work," said Ernie flatly, and the strength of his conviction suddenly helped me to see that there might well be some personal biography at work here—and, in truth, Ernie would not be the first man in history to take his own subjective experience as Holy Writ.

When I categorise my Christian friends, mentally, according to whether they're Protestant or Catholic, I immediately run into the difficulty that many of them are not church-goers in either tradition, though most were reared in one or the other. If I didn't already know my friends' various backgrounds, moreover, I'd have a tough time deciding to which communion they belong. The Catholics certainly don't seem any more moral than the Protestants, and the Protestants don't seem any more free-thinking than the Catholics. Even attitudes toward some of the touchstone issues—contraception, abortion—don't divide neatly along denominational lines.

If there is one issue that does split my Catholic and Protestant friends fairly predictably, it's the issue of funding for Catholic schools. In the province of Ontario, Catholic schools are funded out of public revenues, just as public schools are. This means, then, that Catholic families are able to secure a denominational education for their children without paying fees (though of course they do pay school taxes). This sticks in the craw of many United, Anglican and Baptist folk—to say nothing of Hindus, Moslems and Jews—who must send their children to tuition-charging private schools if they wish them raised in the precepts of their own faiths, while still paying taxes to support the public and Catholic systems. Protestants tend to see this set-up as inherently biased and unjust, and Catholics generally don't understand what the fuss is about. I have personally known this issue to destroy at least one dinner party among people who otherwise loved and respected each other.

But, it's worth repeating—even while acknowledging that my own experience is necessarily limited and subjective—that I see no other substantive differences in the beliefs and practices of Catholics and Protestants in my own social circles. I was just about to share this happily unifying thought, when Doug spoke up.

"Our Holy Mother is speaking to me," he said.

"What?" said Ernie.

"Our Holy Mother is speaking to me," said Doug again—the usual lag time conspicuously absent.

Ernie looked at Doug as if he'd just sprouted a second head. "Who the hell is Our Holy Mother?" he said.

"I think he means the Virgin Mary," I said.

Doug had meanwhile stopped, closed his eyes, and raised his arms in the air. A moment later a beatific smile spread over his face. "Yes. Yes. I hear you, Mother," he said.

"The guy's a complete wacko," said Ernie. We stood and stared at our tall friend for a full minute while his smile grew ever wider.

I asked, "What—what's Mary saying, Doug?"

"Take your meds, take your meds," said Ernie, putting on an ethereal, other-worldly voice.

Doug ignored this. "She's saying She forgives you," he said. "She forgives you for not believing in Her."

"Let's just leave him here," said Ernie to me.

Doug gave a deep groan. "And she feels the terrible pain of all humanity," he said. "The terrible, terrible pain. Ohhhhhhhhh!"

"He's going to start foaming at the mouth any minute," said Ernie.

"She loves us all," said Doug.

"Oh, good," said Ernie.

"And she says Protestants will see the error of their ways, and Catholics just have to be very patient with them," said Doug, still channelling a remarkably partisan Virgin Mary.

"Oh, for God's sake," said Ernie impatiently.

"Ohhhhhhhhhhh!" said Doug, giving one last groan for good measure. He was silent for a moment, then opened his eyes. "Did something just happen?" he asked innocently.

Ernie snorted, and was probably about to say something cutting, when another strategy occurred to him. "No," he said, looking innocent in his turn.

"*Nothing* happened?" said Doug. "There wasn't a . . . visitation?"

"Nothing," said Ernie. "Well, you sort of stood still for a moment and acted like you got up too quickly, but nothing else. Do you feel okay?"

Doug clearly hadn't expected this, and he looked thoroughly flummoxed. "I didn't say anything?" he said.

"Not that I heard," said Ernie innocently. "Did you hear anything, Paul?"

"Well, you may have mumbled something, Doug," I said, not sure what was the best course of action. Doug struck me as unhinged enough that he might decide to go off into another trance and start *yelling* his messages from the Queen of Heaven.

"Yes, well, your lips moved a little," said Ernie. "Is there a history of epilepsy in your family?"

"No," said Doug crossly, and the three of us moved on, Doug sulking, Ernie very pleased with himself, and I beginning to wonder if there could possibly be a weirder trio than ourselves anywhere in Christendom.

We were still in these separate and separated states when, after a solid wall of brush, we came to a clearing from which we could see the back of a log house. Viewed from its back yard there was nothing particularly striking about it, but the lawn and garden were well-tended, and a small sign signalled that THE STAUNTON SHRINE IS OPEN.

"What does the *Guide* say?" asked Ernie.

I pulled it out and read aloud:

> The first shrine on the Lakefield leg of the trail is the work
> of Bartholomew and Rita Staunton. Mr Staunton is a local
> potter of some renown, and he has transformed his main
> showroom into a scene of the crucifixion. All of the figures
> in the scene are made of clay from the shores of nearby
> Clear Lake, and fired in Mr Staunton's own backyard kiln.
> Rating: ★ ★

"Two stars," said Ernie. "How do we feel about two stars?"

"Hmm," I said.

"...Two stars is good," said Doug.

"In the *Michelin Guide*, maybe," I said. "But we've seen places with one star, and we wouldn't want to go back there again."

"—I liked the Krupps'," said Ernie.

"Yes, but that had nothing to do with the shrine," I reminded him. "That was the soup. And you must have a cast iron stomach."

"It was really good soup," said Ernie, with a faraway look on his face. He'd clearly realised it was lunch time.

"Whereas," I said, addressing myself to Doug, "we saw a place with a five-star rating, and that was just amazing. I'm thinking that we should stick to four- and five-star places from here on."

"...Do you think Jesus would have been found in a five-star hotel?" asked Doug.

He'd got me. That was unanswerable—and really quite clever. "All right," I said. "Let's see what's on offer." And we made our way to the back door—to which a couple of arrows pointed us—at which we were greeted by a slender and gracious lady in her early sixties who welcomed us into her home with warmth and charm. The reception area was very small, but we were there only a minute as she led us downstairs into a room that took up at least half of the basement.

There's no question that the shrine was impressive. The Stauntons had created a hill out of papier mâché, and at the top of the hill had placed three crosses, the middle somewhat higher than the other two. There was a crucified figure on each of the

crosses, and there were figures also at their base—Roman soldiers and Jewish townsfolk. Each of the figures stood about a
foot high, and the attention given to their facial expressions and
to the detail on their clothing rewarded careful study. Yes, it was
decidedly impressive, but it was also a little odd, just a trifle
macabre. It wasn't what one might remotely describe as celebra-
tory, and something in me felt a wistful tug at the recollection of
Bill Krupp's buses and fish. Weird as that display was, in its way,
it at least reflected Bill's own genuine passion—rather than
Jesus's, if you follow me.

But perhaps I'm reading backwards from what happened next.
Mrs Rita Staunton was, as I say, an elegant and charming lady, but
she was not the potter—and the potter appeared, drying his hands
energetically on paper towelling, a couple of minutes into our visit.

"Hallo, hallo," he said, extending his hand to each of us in
turn. "Sorry not to have welcomed you at the door. I'm
Bartholomew Staunton."

We each shook hands and made complimentary remarks
about the quality of his work. He took in the praise, smiling
broadly and rubbing his hands still, though they had ceased to
be wet. He was a short fellow, white haired, pot-bellied, and with
rather unfortunate teeth. There was also an ancient scar on his
left cheek that made me wonder, briefly, if he'd fought a duel at
some point in his youth.

Doug had been examining the figure of Jesus closely, however, and he had a question. ". . . Why does Jesus have a blue
face?" he asked.

"Ah," said Bartholomew, "that's an *homage*."

". . . What do you mean?" said Doug.

"It's an *homage* to Daz," said Bartholomew. "Her sculpture at
the church has a blue-faced Jesus."

The stunned expression on Doug's face told me that this was
news to him. ". . . Why?" he asked.

"She'd gone to India, and she was very impressed with Hindu
art," said Bartholomew. "In Hindu art, Krishna is often portrayed with blue skin."

"And playing the flute. He liked to play the flute," added Rita helpfully.

Doug was clearly scandalised. "But Our Lord didn't have blue skin!" he said.

"Put a guy on the cross for a couple of hours and he might have," said Ernie, apparently oblivious of the extent of the blasphemy Doug felt had been committed.

"No!" cried Doug. "He did not have blue skin. And he didn't play the lute!"

"The *flute*!" trilled Rita Staunton. "A wind instrument. Quite different."

"I thought about giving Jesus one in this piece, but I figured the Romans would have confiscated it," said Bartholomew.

"JESUS DID NOT PLAY THE FLUTE!" shouted Doug.

"How do you know?" asked Ernie, just a little pleased, I suspect, to see Doug so flustered—but also surprised by our tall friend's depth of feeling on the issue.

"Because it doesn't say so in the Bible!" said Doug. There was a brief silence.

"Well, well," said Bartholomew, rubbing his hands together again. "Would you each like one?"

"Like one?" I said.

"A Jesus figure," said Bartholomew, and he picked up a shoebox from the floor, flipped off the lid, and displayed a copy of the Jesus figure currently occupying the middle cross. "Or," he said, "I have a Virgin Mary." He handed Jesus to his wife, picked up another shoebox, raised the lid, and showed off a copy of a female figure kneeling, tears running down her face, her hands raised in supplication.

Ernie looked both of them over very carefully. "I could get used to the blue skin," he said.

"It grows on you," said Rita earnestly. "It really does."

I was alarmed to see that Doug had now positioned himself in a corner of the room, facing away from the display, and was looking heavenward. His hands were spread once more, as they were when he channelled the Virgin Mary, but this time they remained below his waist. I could not see his face, but I suspected that it no longer featured a beatific smile.

"I'll have one of each," said Ernie. "Let's see if I can get them into your knapsack, Paul." I turned obligingly, and he unzipped it and began rummaging around to make room. (With four children, three of whom are delicate daughters, I've long resigned myself to being a kind of all-purpose packhorse.)

"That's one Jesus and one Mary at $79.95 each," said Bartholomew, so that's $159.90 and I'll just work out the tax."

"What?" said Ernie.

"I'll just work out the tax," said Bartholomew, beaming away—an unfortunate choice, given the state of his teeth.

"What do you mean?" asked Ernie.

"The tax on the figures," said Bartholomew.

"You mean there's a *charge*?" said Ernie.

"Oh, dear," said Rita.

"Of course there's a charge," said Bartholomew. "I'm not *giving* them away."

"Thank you, Jesus," said Doug, off by himself in the corner. I had no idea whether this was a comment on these proceedings, or if our Lord and Saviour had just answered another prayer altogether.

"I'm not *paying* for them," said Ernie, who had clearly seen the figures as roughly equivalent to bowls of soup. "I'll make a donation, but I'm not paying for them."

"They're $79.95 each," said Bartholomew, revealing an unexpectedly steely side to his character. "Plus tax."

So Ernie removed the figures from my knapsack, and there followed a distinctly uncomfortable couple of minutes during which we did what we could to extricate ourselves from a very embarrassing situation. Not that Ernie was embarrassed: indignant, yes, but not embarrassed. And Bartholomew, for his part, was all puffed up with self-righteousness and artistic pride. But Rita and I *were* embarrassed, and we exchanged agonised smiles just before we began climbing the stairs to the back door. Doug, for his part, was still communing with the saints, and spoke not at all to any visible entity as we made our exit.

"Do come again," said Rita half-heartedly. I opened my mouth to say something equally insincere, then distinguished myself by tripping over the doormat, as I'd done earlier in the day at the Tourism Bureau. I'm good at that sort of thing. If you want involuntary ankle-twisting, bone-crunching slapstick, I'm your man. And I don't even charge.

Ernie picked me up. "Watch yourself there, cowboy," he said.

"Did he break anything?" I heard Bartholomew asking hopefully, safe inside the house. Ernie snorted.

Rita closed the door firmly behind us, and none of us said a word as we made our way through the garden and back onto the trail, which was well-wooded for the next third of a kilometre or so. And we maintained our silence until, some moments later, we came to an area where the trees had been cut back on either side to form a rough circle, bisected by the trail. There we suddenly found ourselves among hundreds upon hundreds of butterflies.

BUDDHA'S EGGS

WERE I A MAN WITH MORE POETRY IN HIS SOUL, I'D SAY THAT there were *thousands* upon *thousands* of butterflies—but I'm not, and there weren't, so I'll leave the number in the hundreds. Even hundreds of butterflies can put on quite a display, however, and these dainty creatures with their gold and blue wings were quite breathtakingly beautiful. We stood, the three of us, in the centre of the circular clearing and watched them take flight and land on the milkweed stalks and tall grasses: take flight and land all around us. When, at one point, Ernie stuck out his arm and held it still, a butterfly lit upon his wrist, and this pleased him very much.

"Let's see old Bart-Fart try and charge me for this," he said triumphantly.

I silently agreed that it was a shame that someone was trying to profit so shamelessly from the pilgrimage, but I recognised that the people who sold me my own walking stick—of which I'd grown very fond—were guilty of the same indiscretion. On the other hand, Bartholomew had effectively trapped us, while the walking-stick vendors had plied their trade in the open air, clearly signalling that they were salesmen.

This whole question of souvenirs is a more complex one than it may at first appear. We who belong to Western cultures like to bring back mementos of certain trips and experiences (though we're not by any means alone in this). In the abstract, I don't see anything particularly wrong with it: making these things employs people who might not otherwise have employment, so the creation, sale, purchase and ownership of pilgrimage artefacts may well contribute to the sum of human happiness. It becomes sad, however, if the mementos themselves are tacky, and if people buy them as manufactured substitutes for whatever experience a pilgrimage may offer.

But who am I to pass judgement? The Poles who visit Bouri-Bouri used to fill their suitcases with driftwood dyed scarlet by native workers (before export controls were implemented in the late 1990s). I've no idea why it was dyed, and no idea what the pilgrims did with it upon their return home, but at the very least it did no harm, and it may well have struck all parties as a tremendous arrangement: indigenous families ate the better for the trade, and these bits and pieces of timber—spiritual jetsam—may have had real meaning for people who lived, many of them, in grey, concrete towers in grey, concrete cities. When I'm tempted to pass judgment, the humanist in me tells the academically trained cynic to shut up and get a life.

"... The richest things in life are gifts from God," said Doug portentously.

"Oh, put a sock in it," said Ernie. He had fully recovered his good spirits.

After amusing ourselves with the butterflies for several minutes, we set off walking again, and it wasn't long before the woods thinned out for a few hundred yards, and afforded us a splendid view of the Otonabee. At this stage too the trail passed very close to the road that ran alongside the river, so we were, for a few minutes, only about twenty yards from the water.

"What's that?" said Ernie, gesturing towards the river. "And that?"

I looked where he was pointing and saw two—then three—tiny boats of what looked like flowers drifting down the river. "Let's take a closer look," I said, and we crossed the grassy area between the trail and the road, then crossed the road, and went down to stand on the shore. From this vantage point we had a clear view of the "boats" as they floated by, and they were indeed made of wreaths of flowers, with a lit candle in the centre.

"That's going to piss off the fire marshall," said Ernie.

"I wonder where they're coming from?" I said. But whatever the source of these floating garlands, there didn't seem to be any more coming just then, so after a couple of minutes' wait we returned to the trail, though not before we'd dipped our hands in the water and thoroughly wet our heads and arms.

"God, it's hot," said Ernie. No response was called for. "And I'm hungry," he added.

I was getting hungry, too, and Doug looked as though he wouldn't be averse to some honey and locusts, but we were out of luck for the moment. In the absence of food, then, we began to swap stories about our respective high schools—I don't remember precisely how we got started. I've found, though, that when men of a certain age begin to talk about things that matter to them, the subject of their high school education often does come up. Is it, I wonder, because so many of us still carry scars of one kind or another from those years? Or is it because that was the time in our lives when the world still seemed ripe with promise and potential? And are those possibilities necessarily exclusive? Twenty-eight years ago, trying to escape a gang of ferret-faced thugs, I consoled myself with the dream that, at forty-five, I'd have a Nobel Prize. Now, a lifetime later, I'm big and strong enough to stare down a good many thugs (though one at a time, preferably), and I'd be made quite cheerful by a nice review in the local paper.

Anyway, I told Ernie and Doug about the time two boys had a knife fight outside the gym at my school. They had Swiss army knives, not shivs, but you can still do a lot of damage with a Swiss army knife, and one boy was cut up pretty badly. And this wasn't an inner city school: it was as white bread and middle class as they come.

Ernie told us that in his high school every Friday at lunch time two bikers had roared round the main building and pulled into the smoking area. From there they'd sold LSD and hash for about half an hour, then roared off again. On one occasion a group of teachers had come out to break things up and send them away, and the bikers and the kids had threatened them with their lives if they didn't get the hell out.

I asked, "What happened?"

"They got the hell out," said Ernie.

Doug told us that during his grade nine year a girl of fourteen or fifteen had become pregnant, and about six months into the pregnancy a group of other girls had caught her in a bathroom and beaten her so badly that she aborted the baby. "... That's why I want to teach," he said.

"So you can make sure things like that don't happen?" I asked.

"... Yes," said Doug. "I can try."

Ernie was quiet for a moment, then he simply nodded his head to acknowledge that that was a good reason to go into teaching. That was, I think, their one and only moment of connection, but it was a good one.

What a weird time the 1970s were in Ontario: I don't have fond memories of the youth culture of that decade. It seems to me to have been imbued with violence, heavy with threat. It's as though whatever was creative in the unrest of the 1960s had soured or curdled, leaving just the habit of disrespect and rebellion. Is it an accident, I wonder, that so many of my female friends were sexually assaulted during those years? Is it surprising that so many of my gentler male friends were badly beaten up? Would I do those years over again? I would not.

And if many of us have become seekers in our middle years, I suspect it's partly because the gods we looked to then failed so dismally, just as the gods of communism failed an earlier generation.

We want to think that our lives have meaning and purpose and significance, and for many of us, no matter how impoverished our religious training may have been, that requires a search for *spiritual* nourishment, for transcendence, for divinity. And that is why this afternoon of Saturday July 12 found Ernie, Doug and me on the trail to St John's in Lakefield.

"... I've got a blister," Doug announced as we found ourselves once again in a heavily wooded stretch.

"Water break," Ernie declared, and as Doug perched himself on a wayside rock Ernie and I had another pull or two at our water bottles. We were well into our second bottle each, and would soon need to refill them, or find new ones.

"How does it look, Doug?" I asked, as Doug inspected his heel with intense interest.

"... Not too good," he answered, rummaging around in his pack. A moment or two later he pulled out a tiny medical kit, opened it, and extracted a tube of ointment and a Band-Aid.

"You're well-equipped," I said. "Good for you."

"... I need your help," said Doug. "And Ernie's."

"Both of us?" said Ernie, but he too went over to Doug, and we both bent down to inspect the damage.

"... No, no," said Doug. "I'll look after the blister. I just need you to put your hands on my shoulders." Ernie and I exchanged puzzled glances but stood up again and put our hands on his shoulders. Doug then put aside the ointment and bandages, looked up to the skies and away from us, and began to pray aloud. "Dear Mother Mary, bring healing to your servant, I pray, and bless this foot that I may walk another ten miles, even into the jaws of hell. Amen." He dropped his head, picked up the tube of ointment, and set about attending to his wound.

Ernie's face was a study in incredulity and mild disgust. "Is the Catholic garbage over?" he asked. "Can I let go now?"

"Yes, you may," said Doug, without looking up.

"Bless this foot," muttered Ernie derisively. "You'll need a special blessing for your ass when I've finished kicking it."

"...Thank you, Ernie," said Doug.

"Huh," said Ernie. But he didn't actually follow through with the ass-kicking.

On we went again, Doug limping just a little, and Ernie and I beginning to think in a more and more focused way about our bellies—but all of us in reasonably good spirits. "I hope you're not hurting too much, Doug," I said.

"...I'm offering it up," he said, looking very noble.

"Offering it up?" said Ernie. "Offering what up to who?"

"Don't ask," I said quickly. If Ernie found out that some Catholics regularly offer up their suffering to Christ, I figured we'd never hear the end of it.

Fortunately, Ernie was in a distractible frame of mind. "When's the next shrine coming up?" he asked.

The *Guide* showed that there were two side-by-side within about seven minutes' walk. One of them had a one-star rating and was described, mysteriously, as *a celebration of local water mammals*. "They've probably got dead muskrats hanging from the ceiling," said Ernie. The other, however, rated five stars, and was described thus:

> ...The Iamonaco shrine is as gorgeous as it is delicate, and a must-see for any serious pilgrim. The young designer has transformed one wall of her workshop into a large canvas, filled with bright colours and warm affirmations. Several shelves climb the lower part of the wall, moreover, with the widest at the base, and the thinnest roughly five feet off the ground. On these shelves are arranged a large number of porcelain eggs, each painted with a scene from the life of Jesus or Buddha. These disparate elements are united by artful lighting

and by a constantly playing musical soundtrack, the latter featuring harps and flutes.

"Well, we must see that one," I said.

Doug appeared to be in earnest conversation with St. Augustine of Hippo, so it was left to Ernie to signal assent. "As long as she's not selling the eggs," he said. So we soldiered on with an air of purpose, and in just a few minutes we once again saw dwellings. There were, in the event, five houses in a row: the first three did not offer shrines, but the fourth, indeed, looked as if it could be a muskrat shack. Ernie may have intuited the truth: the structure was more shack than house and had smoke coming from the chimney—a most extraordinary thing given the heat. There was a fat fellow swilling beer in a Muskoka chair in the back yard facing the trail, and he hailed us as we approached.

"Are youse guys comin' in?"

"No, we're not, thank you," I replied.

"But I bet youse goin' next door," he said bitterly.

"Well, youse right," I said, figuring I might disarm the man by addressing him in the vernacular. It didn't work: he glared at me balefully, but said nothing more. We sailed on by, and after passing a copse of sumac had a clear view of the Iamonaco residence—a small two-bedroom home (I'd guess) painted white with blue trim. There was a solarium on the back of the house, and it was to its door that we were led by a cedar-bark pathway.

I was just about to knock, when I saw a small card in the door which read, WE'RE OUT: PLEASE COME IN. AND DON'T FORGET TO SIGN THE GUEST BOOK. "Should we go in?" I asked.

"Sure," said Ernie. "That's what it says." So we entered.

We saw immediately that the solarium wasn't simply a solarium, but also a workshop and the site of the shrine. There were generous windows on three walls, but the one immediately in front of us as we came in was given over to the "large canvas . . . filled with bright colours and warm affirmations" that the *Guide* had mentioned. Well, let me demur from that description just a little: the colours were more pastel than bright, but the effect was at once stirring and peaceful, and the artist had indeed written a number of affirmations in a beautiful flowing script: GOD IS LOVE; THE CALM MAN DWELLS IN PEACE; HATE IS APPEASED ONLY BY LOVE; THE TENDER-HEARTED HAVE ALREADY ACHIEVED BUDDHAHOOD; LET US POUR OUT LOVE AND COMPASSION ON ALL BEINGS! The shelves were exactly as described, but the *Guide* had not done justice to the porcelain eggs. Yes, they did feature scenes from the lives of Jesus and Buddha, but this sounds terribly prosaic, while in fact each egg was a little revelation unto itself. I've seen photographs of Fabergé eggs and acknowledge that they're beautiful, but I have to say that I'd sooner have an Iamonaco egg: the brushwork was exquisite, and I marvelled then—and marvel now—that the artist had managed to put so much detail on such small surfaces.

And what of the artist's decision to combine and juxtapose scenes from the life of both Buddha and Jesus? I can say only that it worked. I'm not sure it would strike many of us as the most natural pairing: why not *Moses* and Jesus, for example? Even the most committed religious syncretist has to concede that Jesus and Buddha believed and taught some radically different things (though there are, admittedly, some beautiful correspondences between their teachings, too). But Ernie and Doug studied the scenes carefully and with apparent approval. Doug was humming a little tune all the while he explored, and it occurred to me later that this was either his monster music—the sort of tune Bill Cosby hummed to keep monsters away—or he was genuinely approving, perhaps because he didn't recognise that some of the eggs celebrated Buddha rather than Jesus. Art can be wonderfully subversive: it slips under the defences of some remarkably closed-minded people. I'm reminded of Malcolm Muggeridge's oft-quoted observation that the Soviet Union didn't ban Tolstoy's books because the Communist Party leadership failed to see how their quiet promotion of the gospel message undermined the foundations of a state built on atheism. When Doug saw Buddha beneath the pipal tree, did he think he was seeing a depiction of Jesus cursing the fig tree? I don't know the answer.

There was, as advertised, pleasant harp music playing, but there were no lights on because no lights were necessary. (We could see the light fixtures, however, and imagined how they might enhance an evening viewing.) The overall effect of the place was similar, in quality, to the influence of Rosemary's consulting room. We felt at peace. We felt centred. Just being there was wonderfully calming.

"I can't believe they leave the place unlocked," I said. "You'd think some yahoo would cart all these eggs away."

"Maybe there's some sort of surveillance system," said Ernie. "Or maybe they've got bikers doing their security." There was a thought. The possibility that massive, tattooed enforcers might emerge from the woodwork if I came too close to the eggs made me draw back a little.

"Do you like it, Doug?" I asked.

Doug smiled and hummed a little more loudly.

And so, after a stay of about fifteen minutes, we signed the lavender-scented guestbook and headed outside again. We realised only retrospectively, when the heat assaulted us—it must have been thirty-five degrees—that the solarium had been cooled somehow, and within five minutes of moving on we stopped to swig the last of our drinks. "God," Ernie gasped, "I need some more water."

A NORTHERN GANGES

PRAYERS ARE SOMETIMES ANSWERED, AND IT WAS CLEARLY ERNIE'S turn to be heard. We were passing again through a wooded section of the trail without a house in sight, when we stumbled upon a drinking fountain. The fountain wasn't the sort of stainless steel variety you've seen by the score in school corridors. No, in this fountain the water bubbled up out of a structure made rather like a stone fireplace. It was surrounded, moreover, by a horseshoe-shaped flowerbed whose borders began about a foot from the base of the fountain. We gratefully drank our fill, then refilled our water bottles. Ernie's appreciation was only a little marred by the fact that a bee buzzed him twice while he was filling his second bottle, causing him to bolt suddenly. I was surprised that so large a man was so scared of an ordinary bee.

I asked, "Ernie, do you have an allergy to bee stings?"

"No, I just hate 'em," said Ernie.

"... Bees won't hurt you," said Doug, and to prove the point he tried to trap the bee in his hands. I was reminded of the

Christian sect from America's Deep South that requires its members to handle snakes in order to prove their faith.

"You're not really from Planet Earth," said Ernie to Doug. "You know that, don't you?"

"...My home is in heaven," said Doug smugly.

"Anything I can do to speed you on your way—just ask," said Ernie.

No longer thirsty, but still very, very hot, we decided we would seize the first opportunity to wet our shirts in the river, and our chance came soon. The trees again thinned, and after a few moments we could see the road again and the river beyond it. We had to delay crossing over for a few hundred yards, however, because there was a fence in our way—who knows why?—but as soon as it ended we once again crossed the verge and the road, and clambered over a boulder or two to reach the water. We found, however, that we were not alone.

There were five Asian Indians behind the boulders, and they'd clearly chosen that spot for reasons of privacy. The two men had stripped to the waist, and had waded out into the water. The three women were still wearing their beautiful orange and yellow saris, but they had stepped into the water, too, though only up to their knees. The men were washing themselves thoroughly, splashing water over their faces and shoulders and rubbing their skin vigorously. Two of the women were also washing their arms and faces, though they were doing so much less flamboyantly. The third woman, and the youngest in the party, was launching one of the flower boats with a lit candle that we'd seen earlier.

"I beg your pardon," I said. "We had no idea anyone was here."

"That's all right, that's all right," said the older of the men—a rather frail fellow in his mid-sixties. "I see you are fellow pilgrims, and the river is free to all. Come in and refresh yourselves."

In that instant I saw that these good folk weren't simply cooling down. They were treating the Otonabee as if it were a kind of northern Ganges—washing themselves ritually and launching a flowery tribute to the gods. What an extraordinary thing, I thought: they're behaving as though the water were sacred. But that thought was followed quickly by another: why not? Why not! And who's to say that the water *isn't* sacred? And how much more respectfully might we treat it if we believed that it were! (Though on the evidence of the Ganges, I recognise that this doesn't necessarily follow.)

I feared that we might have offended the women's sense of modesty, but that didn't appear to be the case. They simply moved away from the easiest point of entry into the water so we could come in, too. Ernie, Doug and I kicked off our shoes, and waded in up to our thighs. We then followed the example of our male Indian friends and stripped off our shirts, submerging them in the river and giving them a bit of a wash before, gratefully, but with a gasp or two also, putting them back on. It felt good. I felt thoroughly cool for the first time since I'd left my air-conditioned room at the Holiday Inn.

"It is very refreshing, is it not?" said the younger man—a fellow in his late twenties, and possibly the son, or grandson, of the older man.

"Yes. Yes, it is," I said. Doug, I saw, had surrendered to the experience to the degree that he had now gone into the water up to his neck. A moment or two later and he tipped his head back and began to float on his back.

Ernie asked hopefully, "Do you think he might float downstream?"

"The current's not very strong here," I replied. "Do you want to go in a little further yourself?"

"I can't swim too good," said Ernie.

"Swimming is excellent for the heart and lungs," said the younger man. Ernie eyed him sceptically.

The youngest of the women—the one who had released the flower-boat—came up behind me. "You are also going to the church?" she asked, a little shyly.

"Yes, we are," I answered. "And I figure we're over halfway now."

"Oh, we are much further than halfway," said the young man. "We have come thousands and thousands of miles for this."

"You mean you're not just down from Toronto?" I asked.

"Oh, no. We have come all the way from Mumbai," said the young woman. She was a lovely girl. Though I'm not much good at guessing ages, I'd be surprised if she were out of her teens.

"From Mumbai? You mean you came all the way from *India* to visit Lakefield?" I said. "Ernie, did you hear this?" But Ernie was busy trying to creep up on the recumbent Doug, hoping (I guessed) to lap water over his face from behind.

"This is a famous pilgrimage in India," said the young woman, whose name, I later learned, was Dina.

"I knew it was known, but I had no idea that people from India actually came over to take part," I said. "Welcome to Canada."

"Thank you," said the patriarch. "We are glad to be here."

And so we talked about this and that, and I learned that the family, which clearly is quite wealthy, had recently made another pilgrimage, this one in their own country. They had travelled to the ashram of Mata Amritanandamayi, who is known both in India and abroad as the *hugging saint*. The administrator of a number of charitable operations, Dearest Mother has a second ministry which may be just as important: she spends hours and hours every day literally hugging people. The writer Winifred Gallagher estimates that Mother has embraced over twenty *million* people in the past twenty-five years, giving each of them a chance, as she puts it, "to feel divine love" one-on-one.

"How did you feel when she hugged you?" I asked Dina.

"Like the universe is a friendly place," said Dina. "And I felt all my fears and anxieties melt away."

"And you really believe she's a saint?" Ernie put in. Doug had retired to the river bank to dry off, so Ernie had reluctantly given up on drowning him.

"Oh, no—not a saint," said the younger male, Ashraf. "She is an incarnation of Devi. She is the Mother Goddess. She is the Mother of us all."

To my great relief, Ernie made no comment, though he gladly accepted the patriarch's invitation to join them for some tea. The two older women climbed out of the water and swiftly set up a little propane stove, on which, in ten minutes, they had water and milk boiling. Just a short while later we all sat on the shore drinking chai and eating samosas. It was a most unexpected and most welcome picnic, and we three Canadians were moved by the generosity of our hosts.

"These are really good," said Ernie of the samosas. "Weird, but good."

"This is my favourite snacking food," said Dina.

"I like pepperoni sticks," said Ernie. "The spicy kind."

"What is pepperoni, please?" asked the patriarch.

"It's basically your ground-up leftover meats," said Ernie; "beef and pork, mostly." Dina gave a stifled little cry, but my large companion was clearly unaware of Hindu sensibilities about eating cattle. "A little bit of moo, a little bit of oink," he added ruminatively. There was a brief appalled silence, during which I could just barely make out the opening notes of Schubert's *Ave Maria*.

"Your friend is always making his music," Ashraf said, gesturing toward Doug who sat a little apart from the main party.

"Yes, he's a very musical fellow," I said.

"He's a raving loony," said Ernie helpfully. "He hums during the day, but at night he barks at the moon."

"Perhaps he is needing a good woman to calm his mind," said the patriarch.

"He's pretty stuck on the Virgin Mary," I said.

"There must be very much competition for virgins in North America," said Ashraf. Dina giggled—whether in embarrassment, or because she knew who the Virgin Mary was, I don't know.

As we sat eating and drinking, a large blue heron flapped its way upriver, not rising higher than a few feet above the water's surface. "What is that, please?" asked Dina. We told her. "It is like something out of prehistoric times," she said. "This is a very exotic country." And it is, you know: it really is. The trouble is that often we can't see beyond our own familiar understanding of things, and so we undervalue them. Do you know why Algonquin Park is full of Germans? Why the Japanese flock to PEI? (It ain't just Anne!) Actually, come to think of it, let's *not* tell the rest of the world about the Cape Breton Highlands, or Grand Manan Island, or the Annapolis Valley, or Quebec City, or Stratford or The Forks or the Qu'Appelle Valley or the tundra or Lake Louise or Mount Garibaldi. Not till we make a national pledge to preserve them.

But I am going to tell the world about Lakefield.

When the picnic was over, and everything cleared away—and I'm ashamed to say that the women did all the work—we said our thank yous and goodbyes and got back on the trail again. Our friends from India, it developed, were actually driving to Lakefield via the river road. Their car was parked at a lock just a couple of hundred yards away from where we'd met them.

"Well, that's an easy way of doing it," said Ernie, once we were out of earshot.

"It seems a bit of a shame," I said. "They'll miss out on all the home shrines."

"Aren't there some in Lakefield?" asked Ernie. And of course there were, and are, and some of them are very much worth visiting.

"... They were very nice people," said Doug. "I gave them a present."

"Did you?" I said. I hadn't seen him do so.

"... I slipped a rosary into their teapot," said Doug.

"What's a rosary?" asked Ernie.

"It's a string of prayer beads," I said.

"Oh, well, that's useful," said Ernie. "And the teapot was a great place to put it, Doug."

"... I thought so, too," said Doug. Was Ernie's irony lost on him? Or was his apparent innocence a strategic ploy? Again, I don't know.

The sun was merciless: this was certainly the hottest day of the summer so far, and probably the hottest day I'd ever chosen to experience outside, so the good effects of our dip passed fairly quickly. Our current section of the trail was mainly scrubland; there were shrubs and tall grasses and the odd stunted tree around us, but we could see over them, and the next belt of forest was still a few minutes away. We could see neither the road nor the Otonabee River, though we could hear cars driving along the road from time to time. We were somewhat surprised, then, when the trail was bisected by a muddy driveway leading from our left (the river side) and continuing on to a big hole in the ground.

"What's that?" said Ernie—not for the first time.

Men like to inspect construction sites, and strange as the three of us were in some respects, we were fairly typical in this one. We left the trail, followed the driveway for a handful of paces, and stared down into the hole. It was about two storeys deep. "Looks like a basement," I said wisely.

"It's deep for a basement," said Ernie. "Unless they're building a bomb shelter underneath it."

"Maybe Saddam's moving here," I said. The Iraqi dictator was very much on people's minds at that time. Ernie grunted dismissively.

Whenever I see a big hole, I think of my ex-wife, Samantha. Just outside the village of Marmora, in eastern Ontario, there's a big, ugly hole in the earth—the biggest I've ever seen. It is, in fact, a quarry: the Marmora quarry. Once, in my late thirties, shortly after my marriage broke down, I was driving from Peterborough to Ottawa, and I stopped there to stretch my legs and just stare down into the hole from a viewing platform. My ex-wife had taken a cultural studies course at Trent while we were still married, and the professor had arranged a field trip to come to see this thing. She had raved about it for weeks afterwards, describing it as *mysterious* and *awe-inspiring*, and while I'd not visited it then, despite her encouragement, I felt I owed it to the ashes of our marriage to see what she'd been so worked up about.

I parked my car, made my way through the monster tires that served as a kind of barrier, and found a Hell's Angel already enjoying the view.

By way of greeting, the biker said, "Fuckin' amazin', eh?"

"It's certainly a big hole," I agreed. That's all I saw.

"Biggest goddamn pisspot in the world. I stop here whenever I'm drivin' by." And my tattooed friend spat, unzipped himself, and urinated defiantly into the pit.

"There's a woman I think you should meet," I said.

"Eh?" said the biker.

"A woman. I'll give you her phone number."

"She like this place, too?"

"She thinks it's fucking amazing," I said sadly.

I told this story to Ernie and Doug as we stood and stared into the hole in front of us. They heard me out in silence, then Doug piped up. "...I met the Virgin Mary in Marmora," he said.

"Not at the Marmora quarry," I said. But, in fact, I was pretty sure I knew where Doug had gone. For a tiny community, Marmora has two significant attractions: the quarry, if you like great big holes, and the Greensides' Farm, if you're seeking a religious experience. A very nice older couple, the Greensides set up fourteen Stations of the Cross, a peace path, a rosary trail and an Our Lady of Lourdes grotto on their large property just outside Marmora, after being persuaded that they had seen the sun spinning in the sky, and the features of Our Blessed Mother in a cloud formation. When word spread of these visions, thousands and thousands of pious Catholics began arriving every weekend, often in tour buses, to experience these things for themselves. Somehow I wasn't surprised that Doug had been among them.

"...Not at the *quarry*," said Doug witheringly. "At the Farm. At the Greensides' Farm."

"We're not interested," said Ernie, but he said it half-heartedly.

"...It was at the Fourteenth Station," said Doug. "She was walking ahead of me, and I thought she was just another visitor.

She was dressed in a sort of black cloak with a hood, and I couldn't see her face. We both stood looking at the Station, and praying, and then she turned and looked at me, and I knew it was Our Holy Mother."

"Did she have a sign around her neck?" asked Ernie.

". . . She was weeping for her son," said Doug. "And weeping for all of us, too. And I sunk to my knees and pressed my forehead against the earth, and when I looked up . . . she was gone."

"And now she talks with you regularly?" I asked.

Doug was silent for a moment. ". . . No," he said. "But sometimes she whispers to my heart."

I still think Doug was a bit odd, but, as I said earlier, I liked him. And there have been many, many times in *my* life when I've wished that Mary, or an Angel, or Jesus, or God Himself, might whisper to my heart. And maybe, just maybe, one of them has, and I've been too preoccupied with worldly things to hear properly. And maybe, just maybe, this journey was an unconscious attempt to clear my mind and open my heart so I might hear more clearly. And maybe I'm deluding myself.

But I don't think I am.

THE HAMLET OF FRODO

ABOUT A KILOMETRE PAST THE MUDDY DRIVEWAY, THE PILGRIM is faced with a decision. She may either stick to the main Rotary Greenway Trail and proceed directly to Lakefield, or she may branch east—which is to say right—over a drumlin to the Hamlet of Frodo. I note in passing that the hamlet is marked on the map in *Lakefield Pilgrimage* (which I've been calling the *Guide*), but not on the map published by the Kawartha Tourism Bureau. I don't know why that should be, and I can attest that it's an utterly charming place and it would be a real shame to miss it. But I'm getting ahead of myself.

Doug had not known about this possible detour, and expressed some consternation when I recommended it. "...It isn't on *my* map," he said, brandishing his KTB pamphlet.

Ernie, who might otherwise have been resistant to extra exercise, gleefully (if short-sightedly) took the contrary position. "A lot of things aren't on *your* map," he said, "because they don't have good maps in outer space."

Whereupon Doug displayed a shrewdness—and I think it

really was shrewdness this time—that I truly admired: ". . . All right," he said.

"What?" said Ernie.

". . . All right," said Doug. "We'll go. But it's going to be tough for some of us." I've previously described Doug as very tall, and I should add now that he was very well conditioned and that Ernie and I weren't. The implications of this dawned suddenly on Ernie as he looked up from the rail-track levelness of the trail to the steep path up and over the drumlin. Doug and I could both see the wheels turning.

"Well," said Ernie, clearly about to change his mind.

"—No, no, I think you're right," said Doug, the time lag vanquished once again. "It will be fun to see the Hamlet of Frodo, and I'm sure there's a fine shrine there. And the exercise will be good for us." And for the first time on our trip Doug actually took the lead, leaving us little alternative but to follow him, which we did, huffing and puffing as the elevation increased, with Ernie muttering horrible threats and imprecations of one kind or another.

Drumlins are tear-shaped hills created by glacial action: the Peterborough area has a number of them, two on the Trent property alone. Not all drumlins are steep-sided, but this one certainly was. We climbed and we climbed and we climbed, and it was very hot, and we were very sticky. If Doug had paused to allow us some rest I would probably have suggested that we should, after all, take the direct route to Lakefield, but Doug did not pause, and we did not rest, until we reached the top of the hill—I was roughly a minute behind Doug, and Ernie about the same distance behind me. When Ernie arrived he had breath enough to say, simply, *bastard*, in Doug's general direction, then he collapsed on his back, his chest heaving.

". . . Nice little walk," said Doug serenely.

Eventually, Ernie said, ". . . I hate you."

I too had been recovering, but I had noticed a sweet smell even as we approached the top of the drumlin, and it wasn't the sweetness of wild flowers. When I'd recovered enough to look around I did just that, and saw, about twenty yards away, a friendly looking black fellow in dreadlocks. He was smoking a joint, and enjoying both the view and our involuntary clowning. "Hallo," I said, and gave him a half wave.

"Hallo, man," said the black gentleman, and he rose in a leisurely sort of way and closed the distance between us. "Would anyone like a hit?" he asked.

"Yeah—of oxygen," said Ernie, waving the joint away. Doug and I also declined, though I confess there was an instant, just the flicker of a temporal millibip, when I thought it might be pleasant to inhale that smoke. It had been twenty-three years since I last smoked up, but something about seeing Trent again had mildly reawakened the appetite. (In the mid-70s you could get high just walking the halls of the college residences.) But, as I say, I declined. The days when I *try* to be stupid are long over.

We introduced ourselves, and learned that the black fellow's name was Desmond. He was working as a mechanic in Toronto, but liked coming to the Kawarthas (which is the name of the area of which Peterborough is a part) to fish. He'd heard about the pilgrimage, but wasn't on it himself. He'd simply come out for a walk. He liked to walk.

"...Where were you fishing?" asked Doug.

"On the Otonabee," said Desmond. "Near Lakefield. The fishing's good there—you know what I mean?" He inhaled leisurely, held the smoke in his lungs, then released it slowly in silky swirls. "This is good, man," he said, offering it to us again.

Have you ever played the game where you ask someone what living person they'd most like to have dinner with? My own first choice would be the former Anglican Archbishop of Cape Town, Desmond Tutu. He's a man of deep faith and extraordinary courage. I suspect he's one of the chief reasons why the political transformation of South Africa was not attended by mass slaughter. I'm not someone who's good with authority. That said, and said feelingly, I could imagine myself voluntarily and humbly seeking guidance from Reverend Tutu. He's one of very few people who seem to me to embody holiness and radiate love.

But as well as being a wonderful man, Desmond Tutu is a symbol of the rise of non-white and non-Western leadership in the Christian churches. On the one hand, that's only just—by virtue of sheer numbers—and potentially invigorating. We seem to have so little passion in our mainline churches in the West, and Third World churches have so much. Their worship is deeply felt, energetic, life-affirming. On the other hand, however, there is a conservatism in Third World churches that's going to challenge and frustrate and bewilder Western Christians. If you ask a roomful of African clergy what they think of same-sex marriages, for example, you should be prepared for a shock. There are lively years ahead.

I asked our new friend, "Have you ever heard of Desmond Tutu?"

"Man, I was named after him," said Desmond. "But he wouldn't like me doing this shit." As if sobered by this thought, he stubbed his joint out on a rock and took a mouth organ out of his breast pocket. And there, on the top of a drumlin near Lakefield, Ontario, he revealed himself to be a musician of formidable talent. He played "Swing Low, Sweet Chariot," then "How I Got Over," then, finally, "Amazing Grace," and it was as though there was a symphony orchestra up there with us: he made that little instrument sing. So we listened to the music, and we admired the view of the countryside—forests, farmers' fields, the Otonabee River and several lakes glistening in the distance—and life felt pretty damn good. And I didn't need the pot to appreciate it.

The three of us descended the drumlin after Desmond's impromptu concert, and the going down was a great deal easier than the coming up. Ernie led the way this time, determined, I think, to show the same quality of leadership Doug had earlier. I did not resist for the very sound reason that, if Ernie came behind, and if Ernie fell, anything in his path might as well have been hit by a small meteor. Doug brought up the rear.

Just as we neared the bottom we saw a sign facing the other way, set up for the benefit of people going up the way we had come down. BEWARE OF POISON IVY, it said.

I have a huge paranoia about two things: having to answer the call of nature in the woods (as already mentioned), and poison ivy. There is a point, indeed, at which these two paranoias intersect and reinforce one another. I immediately began revisiting, in my mind, all the moments when I might have sat on, or brushed against, or pushed past great swaths of poison ivy, and the thought made me break out into a sweat over and above the one I was already in because of the heat. "Have you ever had poison ivy, Ernie?" I asked.

"Nope," said Ernie.

"How about you, Doug?" I looked behind me. But Doug was communing with Thomas Aquinas and humming his monster music, and probably imagined himself immune to anything more irksome than the odd blister. In any event, he didn't hear me.

When we reached the bottom we found ourselves plunged into forest—the kind of cool, deep, green cathedral-like forest with occasional shafts of sunshine that makes you feel it's never been disturbed. Given what I know about the rapacious logging practices of the nineteenth and twentieth centuries I think that's highly unlikely, but I guess it's possible that this one small pocket was left untouched. Whatever the truth may be, it was lovely and quiet and awe-inspiring in a way that great big holes in the ground will never be for me, and the next twenty minutes were probably the most pleasant walking conditions of the whole trip. The sweat dried on our faces, our steps lightened, and we began to look around us with unqualified delight—noticing even small details like patches of wild flowers growing among the trees.

We were trundling along quite happily, when we began to hear, very softly at first, and then more clearly, the sound of running water, and several minutes after we first noticed the sound we came around a bend in the path through the forest, and there was a stream, and about fifty yards upstream a miniature dam, and beyond that the Hamlet of Frodo.

I'm a sucker for villages. I like the idea of knowing my neighbours, the possibility of walking everywhere, the slower pace of life, the old homes and quaint churches and lovingly tended gardens. I'm sure there's a darker side to village life, or to life in some villages, but I want to focus on the positive. Lakefield is a nice village—though I'll have one harsh criticism of it in a little while. The Hamlet of Frodo, however, is a gem.

It is, as I've already mentioned, a community of forty houses, a tiny church (Anglican, as it happens) and a general store. The houses seem mostly to have been built in the 1920s and preserved carefully through the decades. The church is an active one, though it must rely on parishioners from the farms in the area to flesh out its congregation, and must share its minister—Matthew Deacon—with Lakefield. The general store has almost everything, from bread and milk to over-the-counter medications and plumbing supplies. What was once the village hall has been split in two: half is occupied by a clinic presided over by a nurse practitioner; and the other half is the community library and art gallery, open three days a week between 11a.m. and 7 p.m. Frodo is tree-lined, rose-gardened, and welcoming to visitors.

What doesn't it have? Well, it doesn't have a school, but Lakefield is only twelve minutes away by school bus. (There is a nursery school, however, run out of the church hall.) There isn't a theatre, but Peterborough is twenty minutes away by car. There isn't a full-scale restaurant, though, again, Lakefield and Peterborough are close by, and a Mrs Jane Mullen runs a tea room out of the front room and veranda of her home on King Street. There isn't a hotel, but there's a lovely B & B run by the Patel family. And there isn't a gym, but the forest trails provide some of the best hiking, biking and cross-country skiing in the world.

What else is it missing? Poverty. Violent crime. Unemployment. McDonald's. Expressways. Rush hour. Graffiti. Heavy industry. Urban blight. Malls. Wal-Mart. Race riots. Video surveillance. Hookers and pimps. Squeegee artists.

So, it's a little piece of white, middle-class, Protestant heaven? No. It's not that simple. Seven of the forty families who live in Frodo are not white, and the general store is owned by an East Indian gentleman. Four or five less well maintained homes suggest that their inhabitants are somewhere below the ranks of the bourgeoisie, though their lawns are cut and their flowerbeds colourful. And there are as many Catholic residents as there are Protestants, though they, the Catholics, attend church in Lakefield. The beloved nurse practitioner, moreover, is a Jewish woman, and one of the homes on Victoria Avenue hosts regular Baha'i meetings. So all things considered, Frodo is a reasonably diverse community ethnically and religiously, though I grant that the absence of really poor folk makes it unrepresentative of Canada as a whole. But, you know, the place doesn't have to defend itself, and I'm mildly alarmed at my own defensiveness on its behalf. It's a good place.

We were proceeding down King Street and I was fumbling for the *Guide* when we were hailed by a cheery Englishwoman in her late sixties.

"Are you looking for the shrine?" she asked.

"Yes, we are," I said. "But we're also admiring the village."

"It is beautiful, isn't it?" she said. "I feel so fortunate to live here."

Her name was Barbara Tapley, and she'd been born in London, she told us, but emigrated to Canada with her husband in the 1960s. He had been killed in a traffic accident in 1993, and in her grief she'd left Edmonton, where they'd settled, and moved to Frodo.

"Why Frodo?" asked Ernie.

"Because I liked the name," said Barbara. "Ted was a big *Lord of the Rings* fan, and something about the name Frodo suggested village life and friendly people. And so here I am, and I've never wanted to move anywhere else."

"Do you ever visit England?" I wondered.

"Every three years or so," she replied. "I love going back. But last year I visited Tanzania instead."

"Why?" asked Ernie.

"Because I wanted to climb Kilimanjaro," she said, "and I did!"

Ernie and I, both in our mid-forties, had struggled to reach the top of a middling drumlin in central Ontario, so the thought of a sixty-eight-year-old Englishwoman ascending the highest mountain in Africa was a little damaging to our self-esteem. But we sucked it up—and Doug, if he heard, probably offered it up—and we accepted her directions to the home shrine, "Mr Stewart's place," gratefully. "He's recently lost his wife," were Barbara's last words to us, "so do be gentle with him, please."

"Maybe we shouldn't disturb him?" I said.

"No, do go," she replied. "He'll enjoy your company. He needs to be brought out of himself." So we went.

Mr Stewart's place was, in fact, on Victoria, one of the four streets in Frodo. The home next door to his was a modest red brick with waist-high hedges separating the front lawn from the road. As we passed, a pretty young mother was trying to persuade her little boy to come in for a nap.

"Come on, Duncan," she said. "Your teddy bear is waiting, and I've got your favourite story tape lined up."

"I'm not tired," said Duncan.

"I'll rub your back," said his mum. Duncan thought for a moment, then dropped his toy truck and went through the door without another word. It closed behind them.

"I'd go right away if she invited *me* in for a nap," said Ernie.

I started guiltily. The truth is I'd been thinking very much the same thing myself. Hypothetically, of course. In the abstract. And only if I were single. Which I'm not. And don't wish to be.

Mr Stewart's home was made of stone and had a large elm in the front yard. There were no signs on the house to indicate there was a shrine inside, but the *Guide* had warned us of this, and signalled that guests were indeed welcome and received warmly. We rang the doorbell, and waited as the chimes died away. A moment or two later we heard an older man's slippered tread, and the door opened to reveal a balding and slightly stooped gentleman in his mid-seventies. "Hallo?" he said, opening the screen door, too.

"Mr Stewart? We've come to see your shrine, if we may," I said.

"Yes? Oh, yes. Come in," said Mr Stewart. He stepped back, and the three of us entered his main hall and, seeing carpet, began to take off our shoes. "No need for that," he said. "Follow me." We followed him, but for all that his words were welcoming, I sensed a tiredness in his voice and shoulders, and really did wonder if we should be there.

Our host led us down the hall and through a sitting room to a small door which I first assumed must lead to his basement. It turned out to be an old wood-storage room, however—long and narrow—which Mr Stewart had filled with a model train set. But this was no ordinary model train set-up: Mr Stewart had built a stunningly credible village landscape rooted, I guessed, in the early twentieth century, and the train tracks were nestled realistically into the landscape. There was a train station, a hotel, a feed mill, stores and a fair number of houses. And there were a number of churches, too—though one was more impressive than the others. And the whole scene was blanketed in snow.

I asked, "Is this modelled on a real village?"

"It's Lakefield," replied Mr Stewart. "Lakefield in December, 1926. There's the train station, you see, and there's the feed mill, and there's St John the Apostle church—," he pointed to the particularly impressive structure.

"Wow," said Ernie. "This is pretty neat." Guys of a certain kind like construction sites and they like train sets—even if they don't have one themselves. Ernie was that kind of guy. And there was something truly fascinating about the realism and the detail of the scene. It was clear that hundreds and hundreds of hours had gone into making it what it was.

"Just a moment," said Mr Stewart, and he planted himself behind a control console at the far end of the room. "Okay, now turn off the light switch," he said.

Doug did so, and the room was plunged into darkness. An instant later, however, electric arc lamps came on in the village, followed by lights in the windows of some of the homes. Then the lights went up in the churches, too, and from a speaker that was apparently built into the scene itself a Christmas hymn began to play and voices to sing. A moment or two later a train whistle sounded and a train began moving slowly toward the Lakefield station. And as it stopped—and this was the crowning touch—a Christmas star lit up in the night sky (the ceiling) overhead. "Oh my God," I breathed, and the hair on the back of my neck and on my arms stood to attention in the way it does when I hear a singer hit a high note perfectly, or read a beautiful passage in a book.

"So there we are," said Mr Stewart. "My little train set."

"It's great," said Ernie. "It really is."

"Please turn on the light," said Mr Stewart. Doug did.

"I've always been interested in trains," said Mr Stewart, "but my wife got me to pay attention to the places where trains went, and after a while I became just as interested in the landscape, the countryside, as I was in the trains. Ethel suggested I do some research on Lakefield, so I did, and here's the result."

"It's wonderful," said Doug, fully present for a change. "I love the star."

"That was Ethel's idea," said Mr Stewart, "but I built it and figured out how to rig it up and turn it on. I did it for her."

"Wonderful," said Doug again.

"She was the star in my sky," said Mr Stewart, and he began fiddling with his console, causing the train to start up again and begin puffing real smoke as it pulled out of the station. I was watching him, however, and saw that he was crying, and I didn't know what to say. We were all silent for a full minute or two.

"It's a lovely tribute to her," I said at length. Mr Stewart nodded, then took a handkerchief from his sleeve and blew his nose loudly.

"Thank you," he said.

"Thank *you*," we said, and we meant it. We left his home the richer for our visit, and the humbler for not having the words to lessen his pain, if only a little.

"He was a nice guy," said Ernie as we set off down Victoria Avenue again.

"I liked him," said Doug. And then, as a minor after-thought, "I think he had a cold."

THE PRAYER BOAT

THE MAP IN THE *Guide* INDICATED THAT WE COULD REJOIN THE main pilgrimage route via a path that went to the north of the drumlin, though this would necessarily mean missing out on about a half kilometre of the Rotary Greenway Trail. Ernie and I felt strongly that this was a Good Idea. The path began just behind the library, and within a moment or two of finding it we could see nothing but trees all around us. We travelled in relative silence for the next little while, enjoying the shade and the quiet and the relative coolness.

We had been walking for about fifteen minutes when Doug, who was once again in the lead, stopped and stood stock still.

"What the hell—" said Ernie, almost bumping into him.

"Look," said Doug. We looked. And there, about twenty yards ahead, standing in the middle of the path and staring at us, was a large cat. A very large cat—at least, by household standards. A very large cat with a grey coat and a long black-tipped tail.

"What the hell is that?" asked Ernie.

"...It's a cougar," said Doug.

"A what?" said Ernie.

"...A cougar," said Doug. "A mountain lion."

"Jesus," said Ernie. And then, "Does it bite?"

"...Yes," said Doug.

"Jesus," said Ernie again.

"...But only if we attack it," said Doug.

"Let's not attack it," said Ernie. This struck me as very sound advice.

The cougar looked at us for a good half minute, then turned and gazed into the forest, as if he'd heard something. He moved, and suddenly he was no longer there. He just disappeared in amongst the trees. "Oh, Lordy, Lordy," said Ernie.

"...That was a cougar," said Doug again. "I've only seen them in zoos before. And in pictures. That was a real, live mountain lion."

"Amazing," I said.

"Do you think it might stalk us?" asked Ernie.

" .. There are three of us," said Doug, "so I don't think it will."

"I need a bathroom," said Ernie. He looked into the woods on the opposite side from where the cougar had disappeared.

"...Do you need some toilet paper?" asked Doug.

"Um, yes," said Ernie. And Doug reached into his knapsack and pulled out a roll. I confess that my mind was far away. I was trying to remember something someone had said the previous day.

Doug waited until Ernie had disappeared from view, gave him a moment or two to pull down his jeans, then called out, "It's just crossed over to your side!" There was a stifled yelp from Ernie, but before he could come barrelling back through the under-brush, Doug took pity on him. "I was wrong," he called. "It was just a chipmunk."

It was very funny, but I felt sure that Ernie would seek his revenge before the trip was over.

I suspect that we all felt some relief when we regained the Rotary Greenway Trail. Our shock at seeing the cougar had not quite subsided, and our return to the trail found us at a point where Lakefield was actually in sight—or if not exactly Lakefield, at least what's almost certainly Lakefield's most prominent architectural feature, the towering smokestack chimney of the old cement factory.

"What's that?" asked Ernie.

"It's Lakefield's own CN Tower," I said, making a little joke.

"It looks more like a chimney," said Ernie.

"You're right," I said. And, referring to the *Guide*, I was able to tell him that it was built in 1932, in which year the cement factory was closed—making the chimney one of the world's most expensive locational devices. We were coming now to an area where water flowed out of a marsh and into a large natural pond before joining the Otonabee River. The trail passed right through part of the marsh and pond, and over a wooden pedestrian bridge. The natural feature was interesting enough, but the area's charm was magnified by the fact that there were about fifteen to twenty oriental fishermen casting lines into the water, and beside each fisherman was a pole with a colourful flag.

The first gentleman we came to was, I'd guess, in his late fifties, though I find that slim oriental men often look younger than they are. "Good afternoon," I said.

"Hi—hallo," said the gentleman, and he jerked his line a little.

"May I ask what your flag means?" I asked. Close up we could see that there was some sort of script on it. One finds this also on Tibetan prayer flags, but that's not what these were.

"My flag say, 'Honouring Daz,'" said the fisherman.

"Daz?" I said, genuinely surprised. I'd assumed that these gentlemen, like Desmond, were here simply to fish and had nothing to do with the pilgrimage.

The fisherman misunderstood me. "Daz the holy person of this place Lakefield," he said. "Daz watch over it and keep people safe. We honour her with our flags. She give us good fishing."

"Thank you," I said, and we moved on. It occurred to me that we were witnessing something fairly remarkable. We were seeing, right before our eyes, the growth of a kind of cult. It was apparently a benign cult—even, perhaps, a rather sweet one—but how extraordinary that we should be there at roughly the historical moment when an individual was retrospectively accorded a kind of sainthood. Daz had grown, it seemed, from being a talented and friendly bisexual member of the Peterborough arts community, sadly killed in a cycling accident, to becoming an avatar deserving of honours and perhaps able to protect and to confer benefits on those who honoured her. Life is very strange.

There were several children who had clearly accompanied their dads, and they had gathered together to sail homemade boats. One might have thought that this would frighten the fish, but the dads didn't seem worried. A small boy came running up to show us his boat as we approached.

"Nice boat, kid," said Ernie, into whose hands the boy had thrust the toy. "Did you make it?"

"I made it," said the small boy, nodding solemnly. He then reached into his pocket and pulled out a piece of paper and a pencil stub, which he offered to Ernie, too.

"What's this for?" asked Ernie.

"You write prayer, give me loonie, and I put paper in boat," said the boy. "Boat take prayer to the Islands."

"What islands?" said Ernie.

"Daz Islands," said the boy.

"These Chinkies have always got some racket going," said Ernie, apparently forgetting that the little fellow was literally at his elbow. Still, and to my great surprise, he pulled out his wallet and used it to support the piece of paper while he wrote. When he'd finished, he folded the piece of paper, gave it to the boy, then fished around in his pocket until he found a loonie. "Here you are, kid," he said.

The boy took the money, gave a little bow, rolled the piece of paper and pushed it into a small slot on the deck of the boat. He went back down to the side of the pond where the other children were waiting, and after a brief discussion, placed the craft in the water and pushed it towards the middle of the pond. The children watched it go, their faces solemn.

"How will he get it back?" I wondered aloud. Ernie shrugged his shoulders. We stood watching for a couple of minutes during which the boat lost all momentum and became becalmed some distance away.

"Look," said Ernie suddenly. "There's Wheelchair Guy."

I looked and, yes, there was the gentleman in the wheelchair, about a hundred yards away but closing the distance pretty quickly. He was pushing his wheels hard, and I felt a sudden stab of sympathy—a sympathy that may have been misplaced and condescending—for his solitary state and the difficulty of travelling in the way he was.

Doug made a strange, involuntary noise, and Ernie and I first looked at him, then at where he himself was looking. The boat, which had been stationary in the water, was now moving decisively back to its owner, and the boy was holding out his arm with his palm facing up and concentrating as if he were somehow summoning the craft. Within thirty seconds—less—the boat was back at the side of the pond. He scooped it up, and immediately brought it to us.

"Fancy stuff, kid," said Ernie, impressed despite himself.

The boy nodded, then, holding the boat in front of him, lifted six wooden clips that had been holding the deck to the hull. This accomplished, he lifted the deck and showed us the interior of the hull. It was empty. He then handed Ernie the top part of the ship. Ernie inspected it carefully, saw that the slot could only lead directly to the hull, then looked at the boy. "Where's the paper?" he asked.

"Delivered to Daz Islands," said the boy. He took back the two halves of the boat and scampered back to his playmates.

"Well, I'll be damned," said Ernie.

At that moment, the gentleman in the wheelchair drew level with us. "Hot day," I said idiotically. The poor fellow was sweating profusely.

Without preamble he said, "Have you got any water?"

"Yes," I said. We had refilled our bottles at Mr Stewart's house. Ernie hauled one out of my knapsack and handed it to the fellow. He unscrewed the cap and, his hand shaking badly, put the bottle to his lips and drank greedily. You've seen beer-chugging competitions? The water disappeared that quickly. He finished it, wiped his face against his arm, and handed the bottle back to Ernie. Then, without a word, he pushed off again. We watched him go in silence. I tried hard not to feel hurt.

Roughly halfway between the fishing pond and Lakefield we came upon another trail-side shrine. This one was a plinth made of granite, surmounted by a fine wood carving of an osprey looking hungrily at the river. The mixture of materials was, frankly, a bit odd, but it was a striking thing. We were touched, too, by something left at its base. There was a nosegay—a small bunch of wild flowers—and next to it a wallet-sized snapshot of a little girl. There was also a piece of blue writing paper, and on it someone had written, "Please pray for my daughter, Ivy, who has a heart valve problem." And I did. And I think Doug and Ernie did, too. But we said our separate prayers in the privacy of our own hearts. Even Doug.

"I hope she'll be okay," said Ernie.

"Me, too," I said. "Me, too."

Do I believe that prayer has power? Whether I do or do not believe, I certainly practise it, though not in any disciplined, systematic way. When you look at the great sweep of human history, it's hard to sustain a belief that the Creator listens: surely the six million Jews prayed en route to the gas chambers? And the victims of the Killing Fields of Cambodia? And the Rwandan Tutsis? And yet—and yet—the habit persists, even among those who have seen or experienced great suffering. It may be that prayer cannot by itself change the course of horrific events, but can give the strength to endure those events with courage. And it may be that praying sometimes gives people the strength they need to fight what seems fated, and occasionally, here and there, every now and then, to prevail.

It's very much a sidebar comment, but I'll make it anyway because it also bears on something else I've talked about in these pages. If there are three races in the world about whom I have profoundly ambivalent feelings, it's the Irish (largely because of the IRA), the Germans (largely because of Dachau, Auschwitz, and Treblinka), and the French (largely because of Vichy and Jacques Parizeau). Now, my own life has been a cakewalk when set beside the suffering of much of humankind, but I felt some trauma when my first marriage failed, and I certainly prayed for help. And lo and behold! two ministering angels appeared—an Irish woman from the Ottawa Valley, and a German lady from downtown Peterborough. So I'm at least a little inclined to think that God heard, and responded, and revealed in that response a truly divine sense of humour. And just in case my ancestors and I didn't get the joke, I fell in love, some years later, with a French Canadian woman, and married her.

Just a few score yards farther on from the granite plinth, we came upon a skinny, dishevelled fellow whose pants reached just below the midpoint on his calf. Unshaven and wild-eyed, he was staring up at the sun while alternately framing it between his hands and waving at it. From the movements he made I guessed that he was trying to move it, slowly, to his right, though for what reason I've no idea. We greeted him. "Howdy," said Ernie politely, but his reply was nonsensical.

"Remember Apollo," he said.

"Apollo who?" asked Ernie.

"Up there," said the gentleman with the interesting pants. We all squinted up at the sun.

"That's the sun," said Ernie helpfully. The gentleman said nothing, but kept framing and waving, framing and waving. When it became clear that we'd get no further conversation, we stepped around him and moved on. I guess it's no surprise that pilgrimage routes should attract a certain number of disturbed minds.

And so, in due course, we entered the outskirts of Lakefield (population 2800), passing Savage Arms and the old cement factory on our right, and admiring a number of cottages on the far side of the Otonabee River on our left. We were at last in the village where, we'd heard, some miracles had come to pass in recent years. We were in the village where the folk singer Valdy, the rocker Sebastien Bach, the actor Matt Frewer, and the Princes Andrew (of England) and Felipé (of Spain) had, rather improbably, been schooled. We were in the village where the famous writer Margaret Laurence and the beautiful songstress Colleen Peterson had lived, and which the musical group Leahy now calls home. And it was hot, and we were sweaty and smelled a little, if the truth be told.

"I feel like I've come home," said Doug, rather unexpectedly.

"No, Doug," said Ernie. "You come from another planet." But there was no malice in his voice, and I suspect that Doug sensed that, too.

But the weird thing was that I felt I too had come home. It felt right to be there.

ERIC

THE BEST-KNOWN INSTITUTION IN LAKEFIELD IS PROBABLY Lakefield College School, an independent or private school with a student population of about 360. I've already mentioned that various princes and entertainers have been schooled there, but obviously the vast majority of its graduates have been neither royalty nor show business people, though most of them will have had reasonably wealthy parents. It's probably true to say that the place graduates a disproportionate number of future doctors, lawyers, professors and corporate executives, but I've met, over the years, a few Lakefield grads who have taken quite different paths—a missionary with a medical degree, an accomplished jockey, a magician, a wilderness guide, and a Buddhist monk. The fact that all these people had one small private school in common had made me curious about the place and contributed to my interest in the pilgrimage. The school and the pilgrimage are not directly related, but some places do seem to have a special kind of energy, and Lakefield may be one of them.

I grew up with a friend who was, from his early teens, an

ardent socialist, and he maintained his passionate commitment to public ownership of the means of production (and much else besides) until his daughter reached about grade six. In the fall of that year he and his wife began, quietly and sheepishly, to investigate independent schools. It's interesting, and somehow reassuring, that the needs of our own children will often trump ideology. Indeed, even in my most left-liberal days, the serious sickness of one of my children would have sent me to the best doctor, clinic or hospital I could find if the public health service could not meet her needs.

The trail does a bit of a jog immediately after it passes Savage Arms (a gun manufacturer), and heads straight into the heart of residential Lakefield rather than continuing to parallel the river road, which eventually intersects with the town's main street, Queen. Ernie, Doug and I strode along the trail, our steps lightened by the knowledge that we were fast approaching showers, hot dinners and decent beds. At least, Doug and I were reasonably confident that this was our lot, because we had booked accommodations ahead. Doug was staying in a one-bedroom B & B on Coyle Crescent, and I had booked a room at a larger B & B called The Weary Pilgrim on Regent Street, just a few doors down from St John's. Ernie, however, had made the trip to Peterborough almost spontaneously, and had not thought to reserve a room in Lakefield at the other end. This was beginning to worry me a bit, because though I had grown quite attached to the big fellow, I didn't relish sharing a room with him—or with any other male, for that matter—and I knew I'd have to offer if he couldn't find a place.

"...I think I need to turn left," said Doug just after we passed the back yards of the opportunistically named Prince Andrew Condominiums. We'd come to a road we'd have to cross to continue on the trail, and Doug's map showed that he needed to follow the road to reach Coyle Crescent, which was still about a half kilometre away.

"Doug," I said, "it's been a pleasure knowing you." And I meant it. We shook hands. "I hope I bump into you tomorrow," I added.

"…Thanks for letting me keep you company," said Doug, and he offered his hand to Ernie. Ernie shook it.

"Say hallo to the Virgin Mary from me," said Ernie, still smarting from Doug's little trick on the trail outside Frodo.

" … Say hallo to the cougar," said Doug—and off he went, humming his monster music, and dreaming of ways to bring back the Holy Inquisition.

"He's as crazy as a hootched-up racoon," said Ernie, using an expression I'd never heard before. We crossed the road and put ourselves on the trail again, this time walking parallel to Rabbit Street, just a few yards on the other side of some light underbrush. And at the end of a driveway on Rabbit Street I suddenly saw a little sign saying "MRS. COOK'S BED AND BREAKFAST."

"Let's see if Mrs Cook has a room for you, Ernie," I said. Just forty paces or so further on there was a break in the vegetation and we crossed over onto Rabbit Street, going back a little way to walk up Mrs Cook's driveway and knock on her bright red front door. The house looked large, clean and well-windowed, and if the flowerbeds were any guide, I guessed that her beds would be very presentable, too.

The door opened, and a sixtyish lady, who we assumed to be Mrs Cook, peered out at us. "What can I do for you?" she asked.

"I'm looking for a room," said Ernie. Just for a moment, and rather absurdly, I flashed back to my first childhood exposure to the story of Mary and Joseph looking for a place to stay in Bethlehem. It must have been Doug's influence.

"All my rooms are full," said Mrs Cook. "But come in for a moment." We went in, enjoying the cool of her spacious front hall, and she gestured us toward a couple of chairs. "I'm sure you'd like to rest your legs," she said, "and while you're doing that I can make a phone call or two and see if anyone has a spare room. Is it just you," she said to Ernie, "or does your friend need a room, too?"

"I'm looked after, thank you," I said. "I'm staying at The Weary Pilgrim."

"That's a nice place," said Mrs Cook. "What name may I give if I find you a room?" she asked Ernie.

"Ernie Gold," said Ernie. "Tell them I've got a Visa card."

"Back soon," said Mrs Cook, and she smiled and went off down the hall and around a corner.

"Nice lady," said Ernie.

"Really nice," I replied. We sat back in our chairs and drank in our surroundings. Now that our eyes were beginning to adjust to the relative darkness, we saw that there were pictures on the walls. One of them looked vaguely Monet-like, and I went over to have a closer look. It was a garden scene, with a small lily-covered pond in the foreground, and it was signed DAZ in the lower right. "Daz painted this," I said.

"Yeah?" said Ernie. He wasn't terribly interested in paintings, unless, I'd guess, they featured large-breasted naked women. I took a couple of minutes, though, to look at the others, none of which bore Daz's signature. Several of them appeared to depict semi-tropical seascapes.

"They're the Solomon Islands," said Mrs Cook, returning quietly. "My husband and I spent some time there."

"May I ask what you were doing there?" I said.

"My husband was a police officer," she replied. "He died there, and I brought his ashes home. Back to Lakefield."

Another widow, I thought. It seemed to be a recurring theme of the afternoon. So much sadness. So much loneliness. And yet Mrs Cook seemed fine. Perhaps the death of her husband had happened some years before. "I've found you a very acceptable place," she said to Ernie. "It's a large B & B on Queen Street, just across the road from St. John's. You can't miss it. There's a sign outside that says, THE KNIGHTS. As in men-in-armour."

"Thanks a lot," said Ernie, getting to his feet. "I appreciate it."

"You're most welcome," said Mrs Cook, and she offered us a saucer with two little mint chocolates on it. We took them, thanked her again, and set off once more, flinching a little at the heat and humidity outside.

"People around here are really friendly," said Ernie reflectively.

"You must meet friendly people in Kitchener, too," I said.

"Yeah," said Ernie, "but in my line of business if they're friendly, they usually want something from you."

"That's a little sad," I said.

"Tell me about it," said Ernie. He stooped down, picked up a rock, hefted it for a moment, then threw it at a stop sign. It struck me as a rather unfortunate thing to do, but I didn't say anything.

"Maybe you should try another line of work," I said.

"It's not that easy," he replied.

"What about the home security business?" I asked. "You could cut your ties with the biker guys and do it yourself. Eventually hire your own people. Or how about specialising in the pesticide business? Spray trees in the summer, and get rid of rodents and insects year round."

Ernie grunted sceptically, and I couldn't blame him. It's too easy for the gainfully employed, especially those on salary, to make brilliant suggestions to those who are not salaried. I've had enough friends launch (and lose) small businesses to know that borrowing money and building a customer base and getting paid on delivery and meeting the rent—to say nothing of meeting payroll—are tricky propositions at the best of times. I take my hat off to anyone who makes it work.

A rather squat little lady pushing a baby carriage rounded the corner ahead of us. She was pushing it fairly fast, and within a moment or two she was upon us. We stepped aside to let her pass, and glancing back after her I saw that there wasn't a baby in the carriage. There was, instead, a large plastic doll. The melancholy to which I've long been susceptible gained a little momentum. Again, I thought, so much sadness. So much loneliness. So much confusion. I wished, and not for the first time, that I had more emotional resilience—a greater ability to see sad things without taking them in. It's a problem I've wrestled with all my adult life, and it still appalls me how quickly my mood can change from sunshine to clouds. I think sometimes that my interest in religious questions is at least partially fuelled by a desire to find some lasting source of reassurance and peace—some guarantee that, notwithstanding life's slings and arrows, all will ultimately be well.

"I stink," said Ernie, sniffing his armpits cheerfully. And that's as good a metaphor as any for the way I feel about myself when melancholy descends. It's as though all light and colour is sucked from the world, and a grim darkness steals over everything—everything, but most prominently my own sense of self. *Unworthy*, I think: I'm *unworthy*. Unworthy of the fact that I have a lovely wife and healthy, loving children and a comfortable home, and that this squat little lady has only a plastic doll in a baby carriage. Unworthy of my job and my salary when my friend Ernie has to live by his wits. Unworthy beside the deranged fellow who tried to move the sun with his hands. Why should I have, when they have not? And in a world that's so demonstrably unjust, what's to prevent some malevolent power from taking it all away from me in an instant?

For the first time on this expedition I found myself concretely missing my wife, Annie. She is, as I've already observed, a French Canadian, and, as I haven't yet mentioned, a bundle of fierce, explosive energy. I've often thought that if she's at all representative of the early female French settlers of Quebec, General Montcalm should have put *les Quebecoises* on the front lines, rather than the bibulous, xenophobic, self-buggering Jacques, Bernards and Luciens he actually manned the cliffs with. My wife's great-, great-, great-, great-grandmothers would have put the English and Scots to flight with one volley of laser-like flashes from their beady-brown Gallic eyes—either that, or seduced them on the spot, which would have done wonders for the *pure laine* gene pool.

I parted company from Ernie outside the door of THE WEARY PILGRIM on Regent Street. From here, in fact, we could see St. John's—the destination of our pilgrimage—and I should have felt relieved, light-hearted, a sense of achievement. But I could not. I did my best to put a happy face on things, but even Ernie could see through the attempt.

"You look pretty shitty," he said.

"I'm just tired," I replied. "It's been a long day. I'm not used to walking miles and miles in the sun."

"You seemed okay up to a few minutes ago," he said.

"I am okay," I lied.

"Okay," he said, clearly not believing me, but respecting my privacy. "But maybe you should get laid tonight. Give Louise a call."

"I'm married, Ernie," I reminded him.

"That's what you call a non-sexitor," said my large friend wittily. "Maybe I'll see you tomorrow?"

"I hope so," I said. And again, I meant it. We shook hands, and he strode off toward his own B & B, and I walked up the steps to mine.

My hostess, a pleasant, middle-aged Korean lady called Mrs Su, had seen me coming, and she opened the door as I approached. "Are you Mr Mason?" she asked.

"I am," I said, doing my best to push my sadness away. I smiled wanly at her.

"Please to come in," she said, smiling warmly and bowing while holding the door open. I entered, and as my eyes adjusted to the indoor light saw that the entry hall was dominated by a huge painting of a cherry tree. At the foot of the painting was a high, small-topped table, and on the table was a bowl of cherries. It made for a striking effect.

"Beautiful painting," I said.

Mrs Su bowed again. "Pleased to show you to your room," she said. "Perhaps you like to take shower and relax?" It was tactfully done, and her delicacy lessened the mortification I might otherwise have felt.

"I'd like that very much," I said, and followed her trim form up the stairs, admiring the fact that she moved almost soundlessly.

"This your room, Mr Mason," she said, opening a door and ushering me into a beautiful room done up in white furnishings—which, I thought, suggested a degree of trust in her guests' cleanliness that I wasn't sure I'd feel were I in her place. "I hope you are comfortable here."

"I'm sure I'll be very comfortable," I said, and eased my pack off and put it down beside the bed.

"The bathroom for the men is down the hall, on the left," said Mrs Su. "Bathroom on the right is for women only."

I nodded. "Okay," I said. "I can feel that shower already."

"I will be serving tea and cookies and some things later tonight," she said. "Please feel free to use downstairs sitting room any time. It is for all our guests."

"Thank you," I said, and we bowed to each other, which I think is a splendid, civilised custom. She left. I took a moment or two to look round the room, located a towel on the rack behind the door, and saw that there was no television but that there was an expensive-looking radio. I went to the window and looked out: the back yard was generous by Toronto standards—maybe 50 by 100 feet. Almost right in the middle of the lawn stood a large and noble sunburst locust, its green and yellow leaves radiant in the late afternoon sun. I gazed at it for a good two or three minutes. Low as I was, I could see its beauty. Then I left the room and headed for the bathroom down the hall.

The bathroom door was closed, which I'd expected, and locked, which threw me briefly. I'd had my heart set on a long, hot shower. Whoever was inside, however, heard me turn the handle, and called out, in an Irish brogue, "Just be a second." So I waited, vaguely listening to the taps being turned on and off. When the door opened, I found myself looking at a small fellow in his mid-sixties. His eyes were bright and his manner lively—but I wondered at first if he might be a little crazy.

"I have explosive bowel movements!" he said.

"Oh," I said, not knowing quite what to do with this revelation.

"The coffee doesn't help," he added.

"I shouldn't think it would," I said sympathetically.

"I hope I haven't thoroughly polluted the atmosphere," he said, and he marched off to what I assumed to be his room.

I entered the bathroom, locked the door, and soon surrendered to the glories of stinging hot water and rich soapy lather.

And while it didn't cure me of my sadness, it and the image of the tree helped to arrest my slide.

After I'd showered, towelled off and changed into a clean outfit back in my room, I thought I might as well check out the sitting room downstairs. It was sixish, and I was already hungry, but the meal was likely to be the highlight of my evening so I didn't want it over too soon. I went downstairs.

The Irish gentleman was ensconced in an armchair, reading a copy of the *Lakefield Herald*: VILLAGE INN GETS COUNCIL APPROVAL, SMITH SEEKS RE-ELECTION IN LAKEFIELD, PILGRIM-AGE NUMBERS RISE AGAIN, blared the headlines. He looked at me severely over the top of his reading glasses. "Are you clean, then?" he asked.

"Yes, I am," I said.

"Don't hold with showers meself," he said. "They make me itchy."

"Ah," I said.

"Not that I'm dirty, mind," he said. "I give meself a good wash with a flannel every couple of days or so."

"Good," I said. I wasn't sure what else I could usefully say.

Putting aside his newspaper he asked, "Have you ever had a colonic irrigation?"

"No," I admitted.

"My family used to go for them regularly back in the old country," he said, getting a faraway look in his eyes.

"We used to go on picnics," I said. And then, in the hopes of diverting him from issues of hygiene, "I'm Paul."

"I'm Eric. Eric Adams," said he, and we shook hands.

"You're not related to the Sinn Fein politician, are you?" I asked. It was a long shot, but you never knew.

He snorted. "No," he said. "He's shite. They're all shite. Liars, the lot of them—on all sides. That's why I'm here."

"In Lakefield?" I asked.

"In Canada!" said Mr Adams. "I live here now."

But the reality was a little more complicated than that, it turned out. By ways and means he did not divulge, Mr Adams lived in the Windsor area, but also maintained a modest cottage in Northern Ireland. He was also able to travel quite widely, and had recently made a pilgrimage to Saint Patrick's Purgatory—Lough Derg—in County Donegal in the Irish Republic.

"Ach, that was a trying time, let me tell you," he said. "We Irish have a gift for inflicting misery on ourselves."

"Isn't it all the fault of the English?" I asked.

"The English?" said Mr Adams, clearly surprised. "No, you can't blame the English for Lough Derg. It's a Catholic place, so. They don't let you eat for three days, and you have to stay awake for the first twenty-four hours you're there, and it's bone-numbing cold, and you have to kneel on rocks to say your prayers."

"It sounds awful," I said sympathetically.

"It was great!" said Mr Adams indignantly. "Best three days of me life." And he proceeded to tell me all about his experience there, which sounded fascinating, though it didn't seem the sort of thing I'd much enjoy.

"Enjoyment's not the point!" said Eric, looking at me severely. "It cleans the soul, like. And a young man like yourself probably needs a good soul-cleaning."

I was torn between pleasure at being called a young man, and mild chagrin at his presumption. After a moment's reflection, however, I let the chagrin go—God knows, his assumption was accurate enough, and my soul could use a good spring-cleaning. I've often felt there must be something extraordinarily liberating about the Catholic rite of confession. How marvellous it must be to be absolved—or, in any event, to *feel* absolved—of all the miserable things one has done, deliberately or inadvertently. "You're right," I said. "It would do me good."

Mrs Su came into the room smiling pleasantly. "Would you gentlemen like tea?" she asked.

"I don't suppose you'd be having any whiskey about the house?" said Eric.

"Whiskey?" said Mrs Su. "No, no whiskey." She laughed merrily. "Lots of tea."

"Not for me just now, Mrs Su," I said. "I think I'm heading out for some dinner. Could you recommend a decent place?"

Mrs Su trotted out the options, and I eventually decided on a Chinese restaurant on Queen Street, with the improbable name of Thousand Flowers Café. "It look very dull," Mrs Su said, "but the food is very good." I asked Eric if he'd like to come with me, but he said he wanted to finish the paper and perhaps have a little nap before he ate, so I bade them both good-bye and headed off to the restaurant, deliberately not going by the church so that I could savour the experience later.

On my way to the restaurant I realised, suddenly, that I was looking forward to the meal, and that suggested that my flirtation with depression might have been nipped in the bud. Perhaps Eric had brought a little grace back from Lough Derg. Or perhaps the good energies in Lakefield were doing battle with— and vanquishing—the bad. Or maybe the statue of a blue-skinned Jesus, so close to me now, was acting like a spiritual lighthouse, stabbing its bright beam through the murk of human despondency.

A GAY MEAL

I LEFT THE HOUSE AND SET OFF DOWN REGENT STREET, AWAY from the church, knowing that I was just two blocks from the Chinese restaurant Mrs Su had recommended. Visions of sweet-and-sour soup and lemon chicken and water chestnuts and cashews and thick almond cookies were dancing in my head when I saw, about half a block away and coming towards me at a steady rate, a portly elderly gentleman wearing a beret and carrying a stick that looked like one of the swagger sticks you sometimes see British officers wielding in films about the Second World War. As I watched, the gentleman suddenly stopped, whipped his stick from under his arm, and aimed it— as if it were a rifle—at a black squirrel in the front yard of the house he was passing. "Bang, bang!" said the gentleman. "Bang, bang!" He paused, watched the squirrel scamper away, then began walking towards me again. "Goddamn squirrels," he said, by way of greeting, and with an accent that suggested eastern Europe.

"Good evening," I said.

"Did you see those squirrels?" he asked indignantly.

I had only seen one, but thought it best to humour him. "Yes. Yes, I did," I said.

"Goddamn squirrels," he repeated. "I wish this was a real gun. Hey?"

"I don't mind squirrels," I admitted.

"I hate them," said the gentleman. "Bang, bang! That's what I'd like to do to the goddamn squirrels. What are you doing?"

"I'm just off to a restaurant," I said. "I'm staying at The Weary Pil—"

"No, no," said the gentleman. "I mean, what are you doing with your life? Hey?"

This was a big question, but it was one that I do try to engage from time to time. "I've just finished walking the pilgrimage route," I said, "and I'm visiting the church tomorrow."

The gentleman appeared not to hear my answer. He planted his feet some distance apart and faced me square on. "Do you know what's wrong with this country?" he said.

"Too many squirrels?" I ventured, doing my best to inject a little levity into proceedings.

"Hey?" said the elderly gentleman.

"A joke," I said. "Sorry. It wasn't very good."

"Canadians are very stupid people," said the gentleman. "They do not study hard enough. They do not work hard enough. They know nothing. They don't know any languages. They don't know any history. They don't know any mathematics. They know nothing. You understand me?"

Under the circumstances, I wasn't sure what I could say. I felt mildly affronted, but more curious than anything else.

"That is the big problem in this country," said the gentleman. "Laziness. Ignorance. No education. You must not get sucked in, for chrissakes. You must fight against stupidity. You must dare to be smart. Hey?"

"I'll do my best," I promised.

"Do you know how many languages I speak?" asked the gentleman.

"I don't," I said, feeling that the conversation was becoming increasingly surreal.

"Guess," said the gentleman.

"I really don't ... three or four?" I guessed.

He looked at me scornfully. "Guess again."

"More?" I asked.

"Of course more," he replied. "I am not a stupid Canadian, for chrissakes."

"Six?"

"More!"

"Seven? Eight? Nine?" His face told me I still wasn't there.

The gentleman poked me with his stick. "*Sixteen*," he said. "I speak sixteen languages. And I am an old man. An old man, for chrissakes. When I die, *phut*!—it's all gone. All that learning."

"I guess so," I said. Uselessly.

"Don't guess," said the old man. "*Know*. Study. Work. Don't be a lazy bastard. Hey? For chrissakes." He pointed his imaginary rifle at another squirrel. "Bang, bang! Goddamn squirrels. What is your name?"

"Paul," I said.

"Nice to meet you, Mr Paul," he said, raising his beret. "Good evening."

"Good evening," I said. But the gentleman had moved on. I watched him go, slack-jawed. Much as I enjoy characters, some of them still leave me floored.

The Chinese restaurant on Queen Street was, as Mrs Su had warned, dull-looking from outside, but inside it was warm, friendly and absolutely packed. I was greeted at the door by a rather sad-faced oriental gentleman. "Yes, please?" he said, and I gathered this was a question.

"I'm on my own," I said, recognising as I surveyed the room that my chances of getting a table were very slim.

"You mind to share?" asked the oriental gentleman.

This was an interesting idea, and one I might once have

resisted. Some years ago, however, I took a train from Kingston to Halifax to see a play of mine performed, and the waiters in the dining car routinely seated single individuals with other people. It made for some richly pleasant conversations. "I'd be happy to share," I said.

So the oriental gentleman led me towards a four-man table where a large native fellow was already seated. "This gentleman share your table," said our waiter.

"Fine," said the native fellow. "Fine." And to me he said, "I'm Randy."

"I'm Paul," I said. "Thanks for being willing to share." We shook hands and I took my seat.

Randy was, as I say, a big man—another big man, come to think of it: I'd guess he was pushing two hundred and fifty pounds, and he wasn't much over five feet six. He had a bushy beard, and I gathered from the pleasant aroma that emanated from him that he smoked a pipe. I liked him immediately, though I'd be hard-pressed to explain exactly why.

"Are you here for the pilgrimage?" I asked.

"Yes," said Randy. "Yes. I drove down from Ottawa this afternoon."

"Did you walk from Peterborough?"

"No," he said. "I have a bad knee." He thumped one of his knees for emphasis. "Damn thing. You know you're middle-aged when . . ." he let his voice trail off.

"Do you know the area at all?" I asked.

"Yes," he said. "I did my undergraduate degree at Trent back in the early seventies." And so it came clear that we had both attended the same school, missing each other by a single year. We spent a pleasant few minutes exchanging memories about professors and students whose careers would have spanned our own. We were in the midst of doing this when an oriental lady arrived. She was as cheerful and extroverted as her husband—for so we guessed him to be—had been mournful.

"Hallo, good evening!" she sang. "I have good news! Two beautiful ladies will be sharing your table!"

"Well, that is good news," said Randy. "The more the merrier—especially if they're beautiful ladies!"

The oriental lady laughed, then beckoned toward the front of the restaurant. Two young women began making their way towards us, and I realised, very quickly, that they were the two lesbians that Ernie and I had run into earlier that day.

"One for each of us," said Randy.

"Well, maybe not," I began—but when I looked at Randy I realised he was joking. He rose to greet the ladies, and I, shamed by his good manners, quickly got to my feet, too.

"Oh, such gentlemen!" said the oriental lady happily. And to the ladies she commented, without irony, "What a gay time you will have with such gentlemen!"

Emily and Ruth (their names came back to me) looked at her oddly for a moment then, realising she was innocent of any pun, laughed. This, of course, had the effect of making the oriental lady laugh again—something for which she needed very little encouragement—and her laughter was so infectious that Randy and I laughed, too. It was, then, a merry little band that sat down to order dinner.

It sounds rather like the premise for a bad joke: what do you get when you mix two lesbians, an Indian, a neurotic writer and a Chinese dinner? The answer in this case was—a wonderful time. We talked and we laughed and whenever our waitress came by the table we laughed even harder, particularly as she kept putting her foot in it. She'd made up a little fantasy for herself that Randy was a Saudi sheik, and she kept warning the girls that he probably wanted to recruit them for his harem. "Men from Arabia very bad, very horny," she kept saying, and the absurdity of this, and its implicit repudiation of any sort of political correctness, and the girls' own sexual preferences made the whole thing—well, maybe you had to be there. In any event, she was quite wonderful, and the food was very decent, and I can't wait to eat there again.

Toward the end of the meal the conversation became more serious, and Emily told us an extraordinary story. She and a male friend had spent two years in Zaire, she said, working with an international service organisation. When their stint was up, they decided to see something of the rest of the continent before they came back home. They spent a full month in northern Uganda and in the course of their travels came to a little village called Uram. Uram had been destroyed not once, but several times, over the previous thirty years—a regular casualty of that country's never-ending civil wars.

When they arrived at the village, they were exhausted. They had begun to realise that it was stupid for two white middle-class Canadians to think they could trek around central Africa as if it were some sort of vast Disneyland. Emily's friend, Jamie, was very sick. Whenever he urinated, he passed blood. His eyes were gummed up. He had an infection in one leg. Emily herself couldn't keep food down. She'd been vomiting for two days.

The villagers were terrified of them. The headmen feared that this might be some sort of macabre test by the government, or by one of the rebel factions that were trying to take over the government. The people could see that they were in bad shape, they could see that Emily and her friend might die, but they dared not lift a finger to help them. No one would give them shelter. They went from hut to hut begging for a bed, but no one would take them in. They came finally to the outskirts of the village on the other side, and they were desperate in a way neither of them had ever been desperate before. The last hut in the village, the most ramshackle one of all, the one that was first torched whenever there was an attack, the one whose inhabitants were the first to be raped or mutilated or killed, was occupied by the last surviving member of the family—an old woman. This old woman had seen her children and her grandchildren murdered. After the last raid she had rebuilt the hut herself, and it leaked rain. She had no one to help her gather food. She had no one to haul water for her. "Come in, strangers," she said. "I will look after you."

About a week later, when Emily and Jamie were strong enough to move around a little, Emily asked the old woman how she'd found the courage to take them in. "Do you know what she said?" asked Emily. "She said, 'Because I love God more than I fear the Devil.' Isn't that amazing?"

It was amazing—and it reminded me again of the old insight, that you will often find the greatest generosity among those with the least to give. And when I look at what a small percentage of my own income I give to charity, and what a small percentage of my time I give to those in need, I am rightly reproached and humbled, and I resolve anew to redress the imbalance.

We finished our meal with laughter, and parted on the sidewalk with many good wishes. The girls went off to stay at what they described as a *gay-friendly boarding house*, Randy repaired to his B & B on Strickland, and I decided to walk a block or so to visit the original Anglican church in the village, the tiny Christ Church.

It bears repeating, perhaps, that I like Lakefield very much and, if Frodo disappeared from the face of the earth, would probably move there as a close second choice upon retirement. There is a complex of reasons for this fondness, not least among which is the beauty of Christ Church and the gardens that surround it. I've inherited from my mother a passion for the miniature, the small gem, and this tiny church, built in 1854 and lovingly restored several times since then, is an oasis of peace and calm reflection in a bustling community.

My one criticism of Lakefield is that its civic leaders have allowed the main street, Queen—which is effectively Highway 29—to become a kind of strip development. You will find in the course of just a few blocks a Country Style, a Subway, a Pizza Hut, a Tim Hortons and a Dixie Lee, and in the summer of 2003 someone was busy building the inevitable McDonald's. There's nothing much wrong with any of these chain restaurants in and by itself, but to have so many of them clustered in such a small area makes Lakefield look like any of a thousand other communities in Canada, and it seems a shame that it hasn't created a streetscape with a personality of its own. Buildings like Christ Church, then, are all the more important because they assert something of the community's older, unique character.

It was still light when I got to Christ Church, and I took a few minutes to wander around the grounds before going inside. The board of directors that runs it is in the process of installing a circular pond and a fountain in front of the church, and I tried to decide whether this was a good idea. It may well be that it *will* work aesthetically, but my first instinct is to think that these elements won't harmonise well with the rustic nineteenth-century architecture. The church gardens, however, are conceptually irreproachable and beautifully maintained.

The board has wisely decided to retain and maintain the cemetery behind the church, and I spent a little while reading the gravestones and reflecting on the shortness of life in the Victorian era. I'm not sure I would survive emotionally if any of my children were to predecease me, and yet in that time it was clearly a common experience. Perhaps people just carried on, putting one foot in front of the other, buttoning their shirts, stirring the stew, planting the seed, lifting the load, grieving—of course—but believing, too, as their faith taught, that they would see their child again in heaven. On a good day I believe that to the core of my being. On a bad day, well, I just don't know.

After inspecting the grounds, I went inside, and was touched by what I found. The board has put a great deal of energy and effort into restoring the building to something approaching its condition in the 1850s, and the church is still used occasionally for worship and for weddings. I've no idea how successful the restoration has been, historically speaking, but I will attest, warmly, that the structure has a charm and integrity that defy easy description. As well as being a church, moreover, the building houses a number of literary and historic artefacts. It's worth seeing.

There was a volunteer guide on duty, but he very kindly let me wander around on my own, and I was grateful for that. Some of the other people who came in did have questions, and he answered them readily, but I was content to read the descriptive cards and look at things for myself—the simple wooden altar, the small pulpit, a collection of photographs of the Stricklands (early settlers of the village). When I'd finished, I slipped a small bill into the donation box and went back outside, where the light was at last beginning to fail and the heat to subside.

From Christ Church, I was less than half a block from St. John's, and I headed for that church determined to take in its exterior, even if, as I knew, I would not be able to go inside until Sunday morning. Christ Church was designed to seat one hundred, though I cannot imagine more than sixty people being comfortable in there, and significantly fewer on a hot day. St. John's, however, is over four times larger, and that's not counting the entrance porch, bathrooms, parish hall, office, kitchen and Sunday School area. The church itself was completed in 1866. It's a stone building, though there's plenty of wood and plaster in the nave—something I didn't discover until the next day.

I admired the building from Queen Street, then walked around the point the property comes to at the corner of Queen and Regent streets, and from there saw something that thoroughly surprised me. While the church was not open to pilgrims until nine on Sunday morning, there was already a short line-up of people at the main entrance. Several of them were sitting in lawn chairs, but a couple of younger folk had spread sleeping bags on the walkway. These good folk had apparently settled in for a twelve-hour wait. I was intrigued, and went up to chat to them.

"It's all right," I said as I approached. "I'm not trying to butt in. I'm just surprised to see people lined up so early."

"Haven't you heard? The Rolling Stones are playing here," said a friendly blonde woman in her mid-forties. (At the time I simply laughed, but I remembered her comment later in the summer when the Rolling Stones played a special concert in Toronto to raise a positive profile for the city in the wake of the SARS outbreak.)

There were eight people in line. The first two—comfortably

ensconced in lawn chairs—were a sixtyish French Canadian couple from Montreal. The lady, Monique, was a little shy, and didn't speak much English, but the gentleman was very outgoing and voluble. "I 'av just 'ad a 'ip operation," he told me, "and it's like a miracle! Look, I can stand wit'out pain"—he did so—"and I can walk for miles and miles. My doctor tells me that soon I will be square-dancing again!" He did a little jig on the walkway, and he looked so pleased and proud and happy that the rest of us laughed with him, and gave him a bit of a clap.

Behind Monique and Maxim were four Trinidadian Canadians: Deborah, a lady in her forties, Deborah's elderly mother, Valerie, and a couple of teenagers who, I discovered, were Deborah's niece and nephew. They were sitting in their sleeping bags playing cards, while Deborah and Valerie gossiped in their lawn chairs. I wondered if it wasn't a mistake for Valerie to sit out right through the night, but she herself seemed unperturbed. "They have opened the rest rooms for us," she said, "and I have a thermos of tea and some apples. I will be fine. Oh, yes."

The last two had brought along moulded plastic chairs: Diane, the friendly forty-something blonde, and Claire, her pretty but rather fragile-looking daughter, each had a book and a battery-powered reading light. "We're Baptists, and we weren't really sure if we should come," said Diane, "but we spoke to our pastor and he said it was fine so long as we didn't worship the statue—and of course we'd never do that!"

"We want to say a prayer for my dad," said Claire. "He's had some health problems. And the Bible says that when two or more are gathered in His name . . ."

"Prayers may be answered," her mother finished off for her.

"I hope they are," I said. I offered to do a Tim Hortons run for anyone who needed anything, but they all seemed well-equipped and ready for the night.

"We'll look after each other," said Deborah. "That's what people do when they go on pilgrimage!"

"Oh, yes," said her mother. "We're all brothers and sisters here tonight."

"And if people get bored," said Maxim, "I will dance for them!" And he'd have risen to his feet and danced if his wife hadn't gently restrained him.

I bade the pilgrims good night, and went a little further down the street to my B & B, admiring their spirit, but grateful for my private room, the pleasant sitting-room, and the hot breakfast I was sure would be served me the next morning. But the day was not quite over.

THE CAT IN THE GARDEN

MRS SU AND A GENTLEMAN I'D NOT YET MET WERE SITTING OUT on the porch, and my hostess rose as I climbed the steps. "Some tea?" she asked.

"I would love some tea," I replied, "but please don't rush to make it."

"It is my pleasure," she said, and she disappeared into the house. I smiled at the sturdy, bald-headed fellow with whom she'd been sitting, and we shook hands.

"I'm Wes," he said, a shade more loudly than was necessary. As well as being sturdy, Wes was a handsome fellow, and I guessed initially that his baldness wouldn't interfere much with his social life. But I didn't reckon with a few character quirks, any one of which might discourage real intimacy. For a start, Wes didn't so much talk *with* you, as talk *at* you; his conversation was more monologue than dialogue. Additionally, he was a powerfully opinionated man: I didn't find his opinions repugnant in themselves, but it was a little disconcerting to encounter such strong views on any subject that he engaged. (After a few minutes it came clear to me why Mrs Su might have sought an early opportunity to vanish into the house.) Finally, Wes was an ex-priest—certainly not in itself a disqualification for close friendship, but it had marked him with a tendency to talk as if he were trying to keep elderly people at the back of a large church wide awake. His voice grew louder and louder as our conversation, and the danger of sleep, progressed.

Now, all these things said, and at the risk of sounding thoroughly milquetoasty, I'll insist that I liked Wes. He may have been loud and given to pontificating, but he had, I'm sure, a warm heart. He was the kind of guy I might call if I had a crisis of some mundane kind—a flood in the basement, a squirrel in the attic. It's not that he'd do anything useful—but he'd *want* to. And you must give a guy marks for meaning well.

I asked, "You're here for the pilgrimage?"

"Yes," said Wes emphatically. "This is a very significant event in my life. Something big will come of it."

"Have you any idea what?"

"No," he said. "God doesn't tell you what's coming, unless He's chosen you to serve as one of His prophets. That's not the mission to which He's called me."

"You haven't left the church, then?" I asked, a little puzzled by the crusading tone.

"The Catholic Church is the only path to salvation," said Wes. "I've left the priesthood, but I haven't abandoned the faith. I just knew that I could serve God more faithfully and effectively as a layman than as a priest. I'm expecting God to reveal his design for me very soon."

At just that moment Mrs Su returned with the tea tray and began to serve us with an elegance and grace that made the fast food experience look like cultural suicide. (Whatever happened to ritual? Why don't we pause more often, and savour life's good things?) I took in the flowers on the tray, the small plate of biscuits, the lovely ceramic tea cups, the hand-painted tea-pot and I—

"ABORTION'S A TERRIBLE THING," said Wes loudly. Mrs Su

jumped and almost spilled the tea. I nearly fell off my chair—as much surprised by the philosophical leap as by Wes's volume. But Wes didn't seem to notice: he launched into a lengthy diatribe against *abortion doctors* and the millions of *lost souls* they led astray every year. It was powerful stuff, and I don't doubt that his distress was sincere, but the subject seemed unconnected to what we had been talking about, and a strange accompaniment for a nice cup of tea on the porch on a summer's evening.

I drank my tea as quickly as I decently could, took advantage of a brief lull in Wes's monologue to say good night, then headed for the stairs, pausing for an instant to wave at my Irish friend still sitting in the same chair I'd last seen him in—but he'd gone to sleep. Arriving at my room, I resolved to do something thoroughly decadent. I stripped off, wrapped a towel around myself, and set off down the hall to have my third shower of the day. It felt a bit naughty, but in the catalogue of grave sins it probably ranks fairly low.

On my way back to my room, my towel wrapped firmly around myself again, I nearly bumped into a lovely, clear-eyed, strawberry-blonde woman in her early thirties. She was heading for the women's bathroom, all swathed up in a bathrobe and carrying a towel, but no amount of padding could disguise the fact that she had a beautiful figure. "Sorry," I said—and then, "Hallo."

"Hallo," she replied, and smiled before moving on. But in that instant, I confess, I was powerfully attracted to her, and it took an act of will to banish her from my mind as I climbed into bed. I was faithful to my first wife, and will be faithful to my second (and, God-willing, last), but physical fidelity cannot prevent attraction to other women—indeed, I wonder sometimes if it promotes it.

I lay awake in bed for some time, becoming aware early on of a strange babbling noise which rose and fell, rose and fell. At last, as other sounds receded, and as the noise itself increased, I realised it was a man's voice coming from down the hall. A sudden rise in volume revealed that it was Wes, and that he wasn't talking, but praying. There was a note of anguish in his voice, a woundedness that surprised and moved me. He sounded alone, unhappy and unsure, and I realised then that his customary loudness and aggressive conviction were just masks for loneliness and uncertainty. Eventually he calmed down, and his voice lowered in intensity and loudness. I said a prayer for him, and fell asleep.

Several hours later, and well after midnight, I was aroused from sleep by the sound of people talking loudly in the back yard of the house next door. After a couple of minutes, someone began to strum away at a guitar, and soon the talking ceased and the group began to sing. That they were pilgrims was signalled by their choice of music, a hymn, but it was one that I didn't recognise. After they'd finished the song, which they delivered raggedly but with great spirit, there was a little more talk, then clearly the group had persuaded someone to sing solo. The voice that was lifted then—a young woman's—was as sweet and beautiful and clear as any I've ever heard on this continent, and it transported me many thousands of miles and several decades back to my own childhood in Africa.

I spent five years of my childhood in the African south. As the child of a white academic, I attended private school, spent a lot of time in swimming pools, and learned how to play tennis. It was a privileged life, and I have often reflected on what that privilege cost, and what damage it did.

We had good friends who gave money to support an illegal bush school some miles from a major city. The school's mandate was simply to teach young blacks how to read and write—skills that the government much preferred blacks should not have. Teaching in those schools required some courage, and attending them was fraught with risk. The schools were run and supported by a coalition of white liberals and Christians—mostly Quakers and Anglicans.

How was a bush school conducted? Children formed a horse-shoe around a teacher who scratched out the alphabet with a stick in the dust. Books were precious; when there were any to be had, they were passed reverently from hand to hand around the horseshoe. Despite these conditions, however, some children did learn literacy in such places, and some graduates eventually went on to secure doctorates at Western universities.

One hot afternoon in the Christmas season of 1964, my family climbed into our Volkswagen Beetle and headed out of the city. We travelled some distance along a highway, then branched off onto a back road. When the back road forked, we took the path less travelled—a dirt track, really—and when that ended we drove for a while on grassland, until we came to a grove of trees.

It was, as I say, a hot afternoon—December is high summer in southern Africa. The event that had brought us to this grove was a Christmas concert. The concert was in part an expression of thanksgiving by the students for the money, books and time that people had donated, and in part a fundraiser. We clambered out of our car and seated ourselves on a blanket my mother had brought with us. And we waited.

The drumming and the dancing and the recitations that began the concert were, we gathered, largely a warm-up for the main event. And the main event was a solo performance by a little girl with the name of Joy.

Joy turned out to be a small, slender girl of about eleven. Her skin was a deep, glowing brown, while her hair was short and curly. Amazingly supple in her movements, she was dressed in the simple white cotton skirt and blouse that were a kind of school uniform for girls in the bush. A guitar player played the first few chords of "O Come All Ye Faithful," and Joy opened her mouth. When first she began to sing, it was as though the whole world hushed to listen. Even the insects ceased their shrill cries.

At first Joy sang with the clear crystal voice of a young girl, pure and uncomplicated. But as her song progressed, and even as she continued with that voice to sing the melody of the song, another voice altogether—a deeper, richer, more vibrant voice—burst forth from her throat, supplying a rhythmic counterpoint to the melody. And as Joy sang on, her eyes closed and her body began to sway to the harmonies she was summoning from . . . well, from her soul. All Creation seemed to hold its breath.

And then it was over: Joy disappeared without soliciting applause, and we and all the other whites in the audience climbed back into our cars and headed back over the dust roads to our suburban swimming pools, servants and tennis courts. While I cannot speak for any other family, I can tell you that we were absolutely silent as we drove home. Words—a layer of interpretation—would have broken the spell we had fallen under.

I have a letter sent to my father back in 1969; its author is another white academic who lingered in southern Africa several years longer than we felt able to. The letter reads in part: "Do you remember that extraordinary little girl who sang at the bush concert in '64? I heard last week that she was run over by a drunk soldier on his way back to base."

The song next door to Mrs Su's came to an end, and there was a round of applause from the young woman's friends. I was far away, however, lost in something between a memory and a fantasy. Somewhere in the grasslands of southern Africa, a small deer was passing through a grove of trees. It stopped for a moment, raised its head, and pricked up its ears at a distant sound in the cool night air. Somewhere in the far, far distance, two sweet voices were singing.

And somewhere in these northern latitudes, there's an angel or two waiting to swell the chorus.

Hours later I awoke again. The people next door had clearly gone to bed, and the world outside and inside was very quiet. I rolled out of my own bed and looked out the window. A light mist had settled over the back yard, and Mrs Su's sunburst locust was lit by a single blue spotlight. It was hauntingly beautiful, and as I gazed at the scene, mesmerized, a very large cat appeared from behind the tree, looked up towards the house, twitched its tail, and disappeared back into the mist.

MISS DECEMBER

THE COMFORT OF MY BED HELD ME IN A STATE OF RELAXED drowsiness until nearly 8 a.m., when the pleasant smell of fresh bread suddenly registered and reminded me of breakfast. I rose and dressed in the clean but wrinkled clothing I'd carried in my knapsack, brushed my teeth in the bathroom, and eventually headed downstairs. A card in my room had told me that breakfast was served between 8.15 and 9.15 a.m., unless special arrangements were made, and I was looking forward to good food and, with any luck, good conversation.

I followed the smells of fresh bread, bacon and coffee to a room at the back of the house, where I found the strawberry-blonde woman alone at the six-person breakfast table. "Good morning," I said.

"Good morning," she replied.

"I'm Paul," I said, and seated myself across from her.

"I'm Eva," she said. Her voice had a Nova Scotian lilt, mixed in with something I didn't recognize.

Mrs Su came gliding in to offer us juice, coffee, tea, milk, cold cereal, porridge, muffins—"But leave room for eggs and bacon and toast," she said. Eva settled for coffee and a home-made muffin, with eggs and toast when they were ready, and I asked for tea, muffin and porridge, sadly remembering the pre-cholesterol days when I'd cheerfully have tucked into scrambled eggs and bacon. Mrs Su glided out again, leaving Eva and me the time and space to talk.

It turned out that Eva was a gardener—a professional gardener. She didn't use the word professional, but I will, to distinguish her from those, like me, who simply plant the odd tree and water the flowerbeds. No, Eva gardened for a living, and obviously took great pride in her work. She spent her mornings, she told me, at a country estate about twenty minutes from Lakefield, working for a Mr Duggery—a retired gentleman. She contracted out her afternoons to a number of different people in the area, and to a couple of churches, including, one afternoon a week, Christ Church and St. John's.

"Is this something you've done since you graduated high school?" I asked, unsure what specialized education might be available for professional gardeners.

"No," Eva said, "I worked as a model for a few years after high school, and then I did a degree in horticulture."

It wasn't difficult for me to see her as a model: she was still beautiful, though not skinny in the way that remains, to me, inexplicably fashionable. "Were you a runway model," I asked, "or did you do catalogue work?"

She paused for a moment. "I was Miss December for a men's magazine," she said evenly.

"Oh," I said. I wasn't sure how to respond to this. If I expressed enthusiastic interest, I ran the risk that Eva was now ashamed of what she'd done and thoroughly fed up with male lechery. If I simply changed the subject, on the other hand, it might suggest that I found her previous profession disgusting. (Which I certainly didn't.) It was pretty clear, however, that the wrong response was something along the lines of "I knew I'd recognized you!" even if that might possibly be true. As it could have been. Though I didn't, and don't, think so.

"Well, that doesn't surprise me," I said—then winced at the recognition that what I'd meant as a tribute to her attractiveness was open to all sorts of alternative interpretations.

Eva looked directly at me for a moment, then, perhaps discerning my good intentions, smiled. "Thank you," she said.

And so we talked, and ate the delicious breakfast Mrs Su had prepared and now delivered. And Eva, like Emily on the previous evening, had an unexpected story to tell—a story that gave me some insight into what she might be doing there. She said she'd spent her first two years on Mr Duggery's estate as an apprentice, working with an older gardener called Lily. She had been hired, she said, to help Lily turn a large and rather weary piece of land into a number of gardens.

Lily had been hired first, and had found the soil sandy, but under her stewardship it became dark and rich, and soon colours sang where before there had been only scrub. "Lily used to say that flowers are silent hymns," said Eva fondly. "I like that."

After Eva had been there a few months, Mr Duggery asked the two of them to turn the last untended section of the garden into a *living meditation*. Those were precisely his words, Eva said. He wanted it to be a place where the phrase *the peace that passeth all understanding* makes sense. Eva had no idea where to start, but Lily knew. They planted roses and dragon's blood and bluebells and honeysuckle, and among those silent hymns they built a rockery and a small pond with a fountain. It was beautiful, Eva said: magical.

In July of Eva's second year she and Lily took a long weekend off to attend the wedding of a friend, and Mr Duggery also went away for a couple of days. The three returned to find that vandals had broken into the house and held a debauch in the grounds. They did the greatest damage to the new garden, the meditation: they ripped out the flowers, hacked away at the shrubs, burst bags of road salt over the beds, smashed the fountain, and filled the pond with rocks from the rockery. It was awful, awful—but Lily did not brood. She felt the garden's violation as if it were her own, but she spent the energy of her rage in healing. Where life had been uprooted, they planted; where the soil was poisoned, they sifted out the salt and nourished what they could save; where roots were parched, they watered. They repaired the fountain, but they did not restore the rockery; they left the rocks in the pond as a reminder.

"As a reminder of what?" I asked.

"As a reminder of the garden's experience," said Eva. "Because it didn't seem right simply to pretend it hadn't happened." And it's funny how these things work, she said. By the following year, those rocks had become part of the character of the garden; their pattern was somehow absorbed into its beauty. They gave shelter to the goldfish. Monarch butterflies rested on them. And the fountain's music was subtly changed by their presence in the water.

Eva paused, and took a sip of coffee. "That's an amazing story," I said.

"Everyone has a story," said Eva. "At least," she added, "I've never met someone who hasn't."

That had certainly been my own experience on the pilgrimage, and I was just about to tell Emily's story to Eva when we both heard Wes's voice. He was apparently coming down the stairs and talking to someone. "No, that's not true," he was saying. "You can't believe a word those people say." A moment later he entered the room, looking, I thought, a bit tense and wild-eyed. Mrs Su entered simultaneously from the kitchen, having also heard his voice.

"Good morning," she said. "What may I serve you? Eggs and bacon? Hot porridge? Homemade muffins?"

"Just bread and water for me, Mrs Su," said Wes. "I'm on a half-fast."

"Just bread and water?" repeated Mrs Su, looking both baffled and a little hurt. "That's not a proper breakfast for a big man like you."

"But that's all I want, thank you," said Wes, smiling as if he were about to face a pride of lions. He nodded at me, then introduced himself, loudly, to Eva. Mrs Su left the room, shaking her head slightly.

If Eva and I had been at a loss for conversation, Wes would have been a godsend. He launched into a dissertation on the church's views on pilgrimage, which I gather he supported, and his own special expectations, which he had every right to, but it was all rather homilyish and sermon-like, and Eva's smile tightened a little as time passed. Mrs Su returned with fresh bread for Wes, and the Protestant in me was maliciously pleased when he covered it in fresh butter: clearly a half-fast was a fairly loose and flexible concept, and I wondered, unkindly, if Wes had taken the same liberal view of chastity when he was under orders.

But the high point of my *schadenfreude* came when Mrs Su was circling the table with a jug full of ice water. Wes was, by now, tucking into his second plate of fresh bread and butter, and just hitting his stride on the issue of same-sex marriages, to which he was unalterably and irrevocably opposed. "THEY'RE AN ABOMINATION!" he declared, and he gestured dramatically with his right hand for emphasis. Poor Mrs Su was so taken aback that she missed his glass altogether, and poured a good measure of ice water into Wes's lap, which, not unnaturally, brought him to his feet. In the fuss that followed, with Mrs Su and Wes apologising to each other, I excused myself from the table on the grounds that I wanted badly to see the statue. Eva gave me a wink over the remains of her bacon and eggs . . . and I bumped into my Irish friend Eric in the hallway.

"Give the bathroom a chance to air, I advise you," he said, as we disengaged, and I thanked him for his counsel, but took the stairs two at a time anyway, having discovered that my excuse was in fact the truth, and I genuinely wanted to see Daz's Jesus.

Clean, hot water has long held an irresistible attraction for me, and I gave myself over to the luxury of my fourth shower in twenty-four hours with a little shame but a lot of satisfaction. Most of my motivation was pure pleasure-seeking, but I'd ask you to leave a little room for the possibility that I wanted to be clean before I entered a place that other people considered holy.

In any event, I showered, and allowed the water to collect in the bath because I wanted to scrub my feet. This was all well and good, but when once I'd finished both shower and foot wash I discovered that the plug was stuck in the drain and I could neither empty nor clean the bath.

I've already revealed a couple of my neuroses, so I don't suppose there's much harm in revealing one or two others. Since my early adolescence I've made it a point of pride to leave every bathroom I use at least as clean as I found it, in the forlorn hope that if this practice were to spread, the whole world would be that much cleaner and more pleasant. I realise it sounds absurd (because several friends have told me so) but I'm the fellow you may have encountered in a public washroom cleaning the toilet seat or washing down the counter or polishing the mirror. Over the years I've earned myself, for my pains, several reports that such-and-such a stall was without toilet paper or such-and-such a commode plugged, some puzzled stares from people actually *employed* to clean the bathroom, and, on one memorable occasion, a tip of fifty cents from an elderly gentleman who said he was glad to see a young fellow so motivated. The discovery, then, that I had inadvertently plugged the bath was, for me, mildly traumatic.

My course of action was clear, however: having got the plug stuck, I had a moral responsibility to get it unstuck. I dried off, dressed, and headed downstairs to borrow a kitchen knife from Mrs Su. Having borrowed one, and having assured her that I didn't intend slitting my own throat (or anyone else's), I returned upstairs just in time to see the bathroom door closing behind Wes. "Damnation," I said quietly.

I hesitated briefly, and was about to tap on the door to take responsibility and fix the situation, when there was a roar of rage from inside the bathroom. A moment later the door burst open and Wes erupted into the hall. "WHERE'S THAT DAMN IRISHMAN?" he yelled.

There's a bit of a devil in me (along with an army of neuroses) and I realised it might be fun to see—or in any event overhear—

an outraged ex-priest take on a militantly anti-bathing Irishman. "He's probably downstairs," I said innocently, and stood at the top of the stairs while Wes went rampaging off to confront Eric.

Eva, whom I'd taken to calling, in my mind, Miss December, came up the stairs a moment after Wes descended. "What's he upset about?" she asked.

"I'm not sure," I replied, "but I think *he* thinks that Eric sabotaged his bath."

"I don't think Eric believes in bathing," said Miss December with a straight face, and she went off down the hall to her room, leaving a sweet scent in her wake.

After I'd packed up my room and settled my bill with Mrs Su, I stepped outside onto the porch and surveyed the street. It was 9.15, still fifteen minutes until the church opened, but already there was a line-up stretching one-and-a-half blocks down Regent Street. The crowd was mostly orderly and quiet at this stage, but it was a startling thing to see on a quiet residential street in a village in rural Ontario. As I watched, a pick-up truck pulled to the side of the road and two fellows began to unload porta-potties—the enclosed toilets you find on construction sites. Clearly, the church's bathrooms weren't going to be adequate for a crowd of this size—let alone the hundreds who might arrive through the course of the day.

I walked down Regent a block, recognising a face here or there in the crowd. Emily and Ruth waved at me; and I nodded to one of the ladies who had come into Rosemary's house just as Ernie and I were leaving. There was no sign, however, of Doug, or Randy, or of Ernie himself, nor for that matter of the gentleman Ernie had christened Wheelchair Guy. There were a number of people in Hindu dress, but no members of the family we had met bathing in the Otonabee. Either some—or all—of these people were in the half-block line that was closer to the church than The Weary Pilgrim, or, much more likely, they hadn't arrived yet.

Upon joining the line, I introduced myself to the two people directly in front of me, a friendly older couple from Kingston, Ontario. Muriel and Michael were both in their seventies, and while they'd lived in Canada for decades—"It's thirty-three years now, isn't it, Michael?" said Muriel; "Thirty-four," said Michael—they still sounded as though they were fresh off the boat. Michael had been a professor of English literature for many years, retiring in 1991 from Royal Military College in Kingston, and Muriel was an artist. ("I do mostly water-colours these days, don't I, Michael?" she said. "Yes," said Michael succinctly.) Muriel was a bit agitated because she was scheduled to have a hip replacement in a few days, and she wasn't absolutely sure it was a good idea.

"There's a gentleman right at the front of the line you should meet," I said, and I told her about Maxim. I promised to introduce them if Max was anywhere to be found when we came out of the church.

"That would be nice, wouldn't it, Michael?" said Muriel.

"Is he French?" asked Michael. *Uh-oh*, I thought: perhaps Michael's one of those Englishmen who thinks the French should have made a better stand against Hitler, or something. A view I take myself, come to think of it, but only express every six months or so.

But I was wrong. "We've had French pen friends since just after the war," said Muriel, "and Michael's always looking for a chance to practise his French. Aren't you, Michael?"

"Yes," said Michael. "*C'est important de tenir l'esprit actif.*" (At least, I *think* that's what he said: my own French is woefully weak.) In any event, I liked them both enormously. They're the kind of people my fifteen-year-old daughter, Nina, describes as "cute": open folk, and very solicitous of each other. Muriel was significantly more outgoing than Michael, but one had the sense Michael could hold his own at the front of a lecture hall. He still dressed the part of an old-fashioned professor, wearing a suit coat and tie even on this warm and humid morning.

A single gentleman arrived behind me while I was chatting

with Muriel and Michael, and we eventually began talking, too. His name was George, and I didn't quite know what to make of him at first. He was a handsome fellow in his early thirties, well spoken and easy in his manner, but it didn't take more than a couple of minutes before he, like Wes, found an opportunity to inveigh against same-sex marriage. Admittedly, the topic was very much in the headlines at the time, but it certainly wasn't uppermost in my own mind. It developed that George was a member of a Pentecostal Church in Peterborough, and it struck me, not for the first time, that the right wing of the Catholic Church and the right wing of the various Protestant Churches have much more in common than they might themselves realise. This will probably strike the typical reader as something less than revelatory, but I think it's interesting when one considers the history of antipathy between the two groups. Quarrels between ideological cousins are often the bitterest. To this day, I've no idea why George was there.

Just a few minutes into my conversation with George, I saw Ernie rounding the corner from Queen Street and beginning to stride down the queue. As he drew nearer, a couple of women—not Emily and Ruth—attracted a bit of attention by stepping out of line and doing a kind of improvised fox-trot together, to the accompaniment of a boom box on the sidewalk. Ernie stopped and watched for a moment, then catching sight of me, grinned and came to join me. "Gotta love those lesbians," he said cheerfully.

I sensed a cloud of Christian censure emanating from George behind me, but I didn't turn to confront it. Truth to tell I was mildly embarrassed that Ernie clearly intended butting in beside me, given that at least thirty people had arrived in the last few moments. Their eyes bored judgmentally into the back of my neck. Or perhaps they didn't. George aside, the crowd seemed very good-humoured, and spirits lifted even more when, a couple of minutes later, a trio of clowns came bounding out of the church and began handing out wrapped peppermints and bottles of water. As they, like young Ali on the trail, refused payment for the water, I assumed that the distribution was a charitable act by

AN UNEXPECTED EMBRACE

IN THE FIRST MINUTE OR SO WE ADVANCED APPRECIABLY, AS THE people at the front presumably moved with some speed through the doors and the foyer, down the stairs and into the basement— a route I knew about from the *Guide*. But after that initial advance, the pace was very slow indeed, and we proceeded in a stop-and-start fashion. Again, I had some idea why. A tradition has developed of circling slowly around the statue three times, in the same way that Muslims circle the Kaaba in Mecca, though on a miniature scale.

The result of the slow pace was that I had the chance to get to know Lakefield's Regent Street, and while I don't propose to give many details, I will say that it's a handsome stretch. The houses are mostly from the early twentieth century, with a few left over from the late nineteenth. For the most part the front gardens are nicely tended, and there are mature, gracious trees pretty well everywhere. St. John's is only one of three churches on the street, and Regent itself is only three blocks long. To reach the end of the line when I first joined it, I'd had to pass the

Baptist Church on my left, and I'd found myself queuing up near the tall and handsome United Church on the other side of the street. As the line moved forward, I eventually passed the Baptist Church again. It's a rather squat, red-brick structure and not terribly attractive from the outside, but I've no doubt its interior is very fine.

Seeing the three churches took me back, briefly, to a summer in the late 1970s when I found myself working on a youth job creation project nominally sponsored by a United Church in the Kingston area. While the church was the sponsor, the administrator was a lay member of the congregation and, I think, a drama teacher in a local high school. Our wages were paid by the federal government. The drama teacher, a Trent grad, incidentally, was a very hip fellow: he couldn't have stood much over five feet in his socks, but he wore blue jeans, tie-dye shirts and sandals, and he talked a lot about getting in touch with our essential selves—which, intriguingly, involved a great deal of communal massage in the basement of the church hall, and long, animated, caffeine-fuelled discussions about street theatre, Peter Brook, and someone called Gurdjieff. I'm sad to say that I remember almost nothing about Gurdjieff except that he gave the world the phrase *being-obligolnian-striving*s, which I drop into casual conversation whenever I possibly can.

Our project was an unlikely one: we were a company of four young men and four young women in our late teens and early twenties, and our job was to dress up as if we were first-century Palestinian Jews (in costumes we made ourselves) and walk around different neighbourhoods in Kingston and the surrounding townships. The most handsome male played the part of Jesus, and when we had assembled a curious crowd of onlookers—something we accomplished by performing a very strange Gurdjieffian dance—he was supposed to deliver the Sermon on the Mount. How this was ever approved for funding I'll never know.

In any event, we soon became quite well known on the streets of greater Kingston, and we began to attract a following of sorts—a group of bored teenage boys, average age about fifteen, who showed up wherever we were scheduled to appear. What first attracted them to us was that one of the young women in our company, who was portraying Mary Magdalene, didn't wear any underclothes, and the *being-obligolnian-strivings* dance revealed rather more than she may have intended. Or maybe not.

So, we would arrive at a park, and we'd break out a cooler filled with cans of pop and hamburger buns spread with peanut butter (a contemporary allusion to loaves and fishes), all of which we'd eventually distribute to our audiences. We'd just be breaking into our weird dance when the boys would arrive, usually on ten-speed bikes, and they'd seat themselves around the area, on the ground, the better to see whatever there was to see. That might have been harmless enough, if a little subversive of our best hopes, but when we'd finished dancing and Jesus launched into his sermon, the boys, of course, swiftly became bored. Sometime in mid-July they hit upon the strategy of throwing their peanut-butter buns at us and chanting, "Show us *your* buns, Maggie!" It was pretty demoralising.

Anyway, on one memorable day in mid-August, a day of sullen heat and sticky humidity, Jesus had finally had enough. He'd just reached that part of his speech where he urged everyone to *love your enemies*, when a spotty-faced, greasy-haired boy near him began the now familiar refrain. He got through it once—just once. Jesus seized hold of the stick that was used by the actor playing the blind man and, advancing on the boy with murder in his eyes, screamed "Get out of my face, you fucking little arsehole!" He hit him six times, forcefully, before we were able to disarm him.

And so Jesus was let go, and Mary Magdalene was quietly encouraged to purchase underwear, and we spent the rest of August cleaning old tires and other rubbish out of the Cataraqui River.

Regent Street is a quiet neighbourhood usually, and I don't imagine there's much coming and going except on summer weekends. I saw a couple of elderly folk out in their front yards, but suspect that most people in the area would have been inside (if they had air conditioning), or in their back yards for privacy. But that's just speculation.

Shuffling along slowly, as we were, with plenty of time to look around and study people, I was struck by how many mixed-race couples were making the pilgrimage. There were many Hindus, as I've already mentioned, but they were primarily of the same race. In the space of five minutes, however, I took a rough inventory of the people passing by and heading for the back of the line, and I observed at least twelve couples whose halves were markedly different in skin colour and facial structure from each other. In a big city this would be unremarkable, but in Lakefield it must still be something of a curiosity. I'll observe in passing that the children of such unions—and there were a few there—were often strikingly beautiful. It occurred to me that among many things on offer from this particular pilgrimage was an implied celebration of social pluralism. Broadly speaking, you'd expect a lesbian saint to embrace diversity, and there must be a real hunger on the part of racially blended families (still very much a social minority) to honour a minority religious figure. This certainly doesn't explain Daz's draw for people like Ernie, Doug, Wes and George—or, come to think of it, me—but if God does indeed move in mysterious ways, perhaps our shared interest is in itself a hopeful sign.

As we drew closer to the church we saw that a fellow with a shaved head and wearing saffron robes had set up a little booth at road-side. His wares were wonderfully eclectic: glasses of cider, jars of honey, a CD improbably entitled "Yes! Yes! Music for Orgasmic Meditation," and postcards of the church and of Daz's statue.

Ernie was in great good spirits: "Hey, Kojak!" he called to the street vendor. "Are you one of them Hare Krishna guys?"

The gentleman with the shaved head smiled in a vague sort of way, but didn't say anything—and that was probably a very good choice.

"Do you think he's a Hairy Krishna, Michael?" asked Muriel.

"He might be," said Michael noncommittally.

Muriel thought about this for a moment, then asked, very innocently, "What is it Hairy Krishnas believe in?"

"Sex!" said Ernie enthusiastically.

"Ooh," said Muriel, a bit taken aback to have so charged a word uttered at top volume in her right ear. "It's a funny sort of name, isn't it, for someone who isn't hairy at all."

Ernie and I looked dubiously at her for a moment to see if she was kidding, but if she was she was doing a remarkably good job of keeping a straight face.

I should mention that just before I went through the doors I looked back, and could see that the line now extended all the way down Regent—three full blocks—and around the corner and so out of sight. Numbers are not my forte, but it struck me that the day's final tally might well be over a thousand visitors. A phone call to the church office a few days later established that on that day no fewer than *2986* people had processed through St. John's basement—a one-day record. That number, incidentally, is a little more than the total population of Lakefield. Obviously, many of these people had come by car, rather than by walking the trail.

We reached the threshold at roughly 10.30, and things seemed to move a good deal faster. The foyer was a little cooler than the outdoors, but the passage of a fair number of bodies would probably change that balance in another hour or so. There was something of a traffic bottleneck, because there was only one set of stairs to and from the basement, though I gather there was an emergency exit downstairs. This meant that even while some of us were going downstairs, others were coming up. Fortunately, people were not leaving by the same door they'd entered through: instead of turning right in the foyer, they turned left, and there was, I knew from the *Guide*, an opportunity to slip into the church for a prayer before heading out the other main floor exit which opened onto Queen Street.

"I must be careful of my hip, Michael," said Muriel, and her husband gallantly offered her his arm.

"May I offer you any assistance?" I asked.

"No, thank you. I'll be fine with Michael to hold on to," said Muriel. And down we went.

Seeing people ascend as we descended offered one significant advantage: I could study their faces and try to guess the degree that the experience had affected them. In our passage through the foyer and down the stairs I saw only about fourteen people coming the other way (simply because the movement of the two lines was roughly synchronised), so I cannot offer anything remotely approaching a scientific survey. I was struck, though, by the fact that the majority of the people coming up the stairs had tears in their eyes. It wasn't all of them, and one fellow looked absolutely unmoved—but most of them clearly felt they'd experienced something important, even wonderful. Not surprisingly, then, our own sense of anticipation grew.

The basement of St. John's Parish Hall is fairly low-ceilinged, and the room itself is neither large nor particularly well-lit. It's evident, though, that church officers have done their best to display the statue attractively. It sits almost in the dead centre of the room, surrounded by a flimsy rope and lit, from above, by a single spotlight. It's scarcely an art-gallery setting, but it's serviceable. It's adequate. One has the sense that the church is trying to make the visit pleasant, without suggesting that the vestry council actually endorses the notion that the statue has miraculous properties. I admire the ambivalence, intended or not.

People were, as I expected, circling the statue, and a couple of church elders were doing their best to ensure that people only did so three times. Their measures seemed to be working. The unexpected innovation, however, was that my Trinidadian friend, Deborah, from the previous evening was standing by the statue and dispensing hugs to anyone who reached for her. "My God," I thought to myself—"She's doing a Mata Amritanandamayi here in Lakefield!" But any scepticism or cynicism I might have felt was swiftly dispelled by the look on Deborah's face, and the look on the faces of those she embraced. There was nothing mercenary about it, and I can only guess that many people really wanted a hug when they saw the sculpture, and that Deborah had intuited their need and was responding to it. I was amused to see that a gentleman in a clerical collar (whom I guessed to be Matthew Deacon) was hovering in the background looking a bit uneasy, though smiling valiantly. He didn't intervene, however, and in truth there was no need to.

Within two minutes of first glimpsing the statue, I was right in front of it. It's an impressive piece of work. The figure stands roughly six-and-a-half feet high, so it's certainly taller than most of the folk who visit it. Its proportions are all a bit larger than life, so one has the sense of an encounter with a large but possible human. The blue skin is, frankly, off-putting, at least for this occidental observer. Jesus/Krishna is playing a flute, and Daz had, perhaps wisely, used a real one. The figure's clothes are also real cotton robes, so I guess the display would qualify as a mixed-media installation under Canada Council rules. It was striking.

While I was still looking at the sculpture, Muriel, then Michael, hugged Deborah. That Muriel should hug her didn't surprise me, but I'd thought Michael might be more shy. I embraced her a moment later, and it felt perfectly natural—completely unforced—to do so. While I was in her arms I saw her mother, Valerie, tucked away in a chair in a corner of the room. Emerging from my hug I smiled and waved—and she waved back. "Thank you, Deborah," I said.

"God bless you," said Deborah.

Ernie had been staring at the statue, but he now moved on—and there, of course, was Deborah. She hesitated for a fraction of a second, trying to read his inclination, then simply opened her arms welcomingly. Mildly to my surprise, Ernie stepped forward and put his arms around her—and then, to my astonishment, he burst into tears. They stood there, the two of them, one small dark woman and one large white man, she rocking him very gently and rubbing his back. It was unexpected, and it was very moving.

After Ernie collected himself, we circled round the statue twice more, then, with a smile to Deborah, a wave at Matthew, and a quick shoulder squeeze to Valerie, I began ascending the stairs, moving slowly behind Muriel and Michael, and with Ernie in my immediate wake. Muriel clearly found going up a challenge, but her husband supported her as, I guessed, she had supported and would again support him in any infirmity. That's surely the way it's meant to be.

When we reached the top of the stairs and found ourselves in the foyer again, we were immediately confronted by the gentleman in the wheelchair. He was parked at the top, but a little to the side, and we swiftly gleaned that he was waiting for a couple of volunteers to lift him downstairs. (St. John's has a wheelchair ramp to the top floor, but not to the basement.) Without pausing for an instant, my friend Ernie scooped the gentleman into his arms, and headed off with him downstairs. He should have asked permission, I know, but the gentleman did not complain, and I've no doubt that Ernie was very careful with him.

For my part, I turned left, went through a short hall with rest rooms tucked away on the left, then turned right into the church proper—a lovely nineteenth-century Anglican nave with brilliant stained-glass windows, plaster expanses painted white, a dark wood ceiling, and rows of wooden pews facing the pulpit and altar. It was the kind of church I'd attended as a child, and everything—from the sunlight streaming through the colourful windows, through the coolness, to the slight musty odour—conspired to make me feel at home. There were about forty other pilgrims in the pews, most kneeling, but a few sitting and gazing up at the altar. Three more pilgrims were kneeling at the altar rail, and there were two people attending to each of them. After watching a moment, I gathered that the six who were standing were members of a lay healing team, and that they were praying with and for the people kneeling—laying their hands on their heads and shoulders. But for the whisper of semi-private prayer, the hall was quiet, and the atmosphere as close to holy as any I've ever encountered. People were praying—for loved ones, for strangers, and, no doubt, for themselves. There was no discord, no showmanship, no ego. There was the possibility of communion with something greater than ourselves, and the fact of caring contact with one another: as I stood there, one of the pilgrims at the altar began to cry, and one of the two people attending her sank to her knees and put her arms around her in a loving embrace.

And so I slipped into one of the pews myself, sank to my knees, bowed my head, and said my own prayer. And I prayed for my dad, my mum, my children—Rachael, Nina, Jackson and Molly—my wife Annie, my brother Robin and his family, my in-laws, my aunt Elise . . . even, after a moment's hesitation, for my first wife, who is, when all's said and done, the mother of two of my beloved children. And I stayed there for some while, allowing the names and faces of friends and colleagues and acquaintances to present themselves, and the names and faces, too, of people I'd met on my journey; asking for them—for all of us— the mercy, blessing, comfort and love that we so desperately need.

When I rose, after some while, there had been a good deal of traffic into and out of the church—though most people had clearly opted not to enter after their encounter with the statue. I left by the door through which I'd entered, pausing only to pick up a tiny blue ribbon from a large basket at the back. My pocket *Guide* told me that this was the one Church-sanctioned souvenir of the visit, and it was admirable both for its lack of ostentation and for its being free. I walked out into the sunlight, then, with a ribbon on my chest, a few tears in my eyes, and a light heart.

A FORETASTE

THE TEMPERATURE WAS ALREADY HIGH, BUT THE AIR LESS HUMID than on the previous day. The sun shone from a blue, cloudless sky. It was no projection to say that Lakefield looked good. I was delighted to see, moreover, that some sort of street festival appeared to be in its earliest stages. A good many of my fellow pilgrims were thronging the streets, but there were also ordinary Lakefielders abroad—or so I'd guess, anyway, by the casual, familiar way some of them greeted one another, and by the fact that a fair number of them were carrying deck chairs. There were also, I saw, posters advertising a literary festival later in the month, so it seems that this small village is an active, vibrant place.

I attended a literary festival as an honoured guest some years ago. The festival director, a kind if somewhat flakey woman, had heard somewhere that I was destined to be the Next Big Thing in Canadian playwriting, so she put me in a room with a seating capacity of three hundred. I'd forbidden my family to attend, so I spoke to a crowd of about, well, roughly six, more or less, and two of them apparently thought that I wrote some kind of bondage erotica (my first play was called *The Discipline Committee*) and asked me some very strange questions in the Q and A period. My ignorance about water bondage was a grave disappointment to them.

Before I explored what this street festival might be about, however, I wanted to see one last home shrine, so I set off on a fifteen-minute walk. I headed north on Queen Street, turned right on Strickland, and then right again on Prospect—and just a few doors down the street was a large, rose-coloured home from, I'd guess, the late 1800s. Wanting to think through the last hour or so in solitude, I'd deliberately made the trip alone, but several other pilgrims had been on the same journey, and eight of us arrived at the house on Prospect within about three minutes of one another. There were benches in the side yard, and a sign that read: PILGRIMS PLEASE WAIT HERE. So we waited.

After about a ten-minute wait, a boy in his early teens came out and welcomed us with a bow. He was, the *Guide* told me, the youngest son of the Cambodian family that lived there. The family had been sponsored to enter Canada by a local church group, and created this shrine partly as a way of saying thank you to the community.

The young man ushered us through the front door, asked us to remove our shoes, then led us through an entry hall and into what had originally been the living room. But none of the accoutrements of an ordinary living room were in evidence: there were no couches or armchairs; there were no pictures on the walls; there was no television or stereo system. There was no carpeting, either, but the floor was a polished hardwood, and our host signalled that each of us should take a tiny rug from a pile in the corner and put it down with the others in a perfect circle in the middle of the room. We did so, and the young man joined us, sitting cross-legged on his rug and smiling slightly. We followed suit.

We were sitting there, feeling mildly self-conscious, facing strangers around the circle, when a graceful young woman in her middle teens entered the room with a tray covered in small towels. She brought the tray around the circle, and we each took one. They were damp and scented with rosewater and something else I didn't recognise. The young man—her brother—took his towel and wiped his face and hands. We copied him. It felt wonderfully refreshing. Our server gathered up the towels and left the room. We were all quiet.

The young woman returned, carrying another tray—this one filled with little bowls. She set the tray down, then served each of us a bowl of what turned out to be green tea. When we had all been served, the young man raised his bowl, and waited until we had done likewise. He then sipped, and by his example encouraged us to drink, too.

Our server had disappeared after serving the tea; she now reappeared with a basket filled with small, colourful, exquisitely wrapped packages roughly the size of a regular chocolate bar. She set one of these down in front of each of us. Again, following the example of our young host, we picked it up, unwrapped it, and discovered inside some sort of sweet rice cake. The young woman left the room, and we nibbled at the rice cakes, and sipped our tea.

But something remarkable was beginning to happen. I didn't know a single other pilgrim in the circle, though admittedly some of them already knew one or two of the others. I didn't know the young man or his slightly older sister, though I knew their surname from the *Guide*. But while we had sat down strangers, and while we hadn't exchanged a word—though we could have; nothing prevented us—a sense of camaraderie had developed among us. We no longer felt self-conscious. We could smile at the people across the circle without embarrassment. It occurred to me that this quiet, low-key ritual was accomplishing a similar small-scale miracle to that wrought by Mrs X, the provider of Thanksgiving dinners.

When we had all finished our tea and rice cake, the young man smiled, rose to his feet, and picked up his rug. We followed his example. He took his rug over to the small pile, and put it neatly on the top, and we did the same. We then followed him out of the room, through the entry hall, and back to the front door—where his graceful sister was waiting with a vase of gladiolas. The young man opened the door, and his sister handed each of us a flower, smiled, and bowed. We left, each of us clutching our own flower, and we walked together back to Queen Street, talking as if we'd known each other all our lives.

We arrived back at the middle of the village to find a street festival and farmers' market in full swing. The police had closed off Queen Street for about three blocks. There were stalls set up on the road, selling everything from apples and asparagus to strawberries and zucchini. A slim, blonde, friendly woman was selling knitted kids' clothes. An older, heavier-set lady was selling preserves and cookies, lemon loaves and strawberry-rhubarb pies. A middle-aged gentleman was selling what *he* called *antique knick-knacks*, though I recognised some of the china animal figures as having been in boxes of tea during the 1970s. A tall, attractive girl was selling jewellery she'd made herself: she was working on a stunning silver necklace even as she displayed her wares.

I stopped and watched a spritely fellow play some inspired bluegrass on his guitar. The sweat rolled down his face and was beginning to stain his T-shirt. "He sure can play that gee-tar," said an old farmer next to me.

"He sure can," I replied, and joined in the applause enthusiastically when the performer finished his song. I hadn't heard bluegrass in a long, long time.

I moved on and watched a boy of about sixteen juggling. He began with three coloured bean bags, moved on to three pop bottles, then tried his hand at four eggs. He was good. I'm guessing from the crowd of kids around him, and from the way they cheered him on, that he was a local, Lakefield lad. "Go, Daniel," said a pretty, bare-midriffed nymphet, who was clearly the Queen Bee of her little clique. He didn't answer, but I could tell he'd heard and was tickled pink by her attention.

An elderly magician had set up a little table covered in a cloth and was performing some fairly standard tricks for a decent-sized audience. With the exception of the smaller children, everyone must surely have seen the tricks before, but they still *oohed* and *ahhed* at the effects and laughed at his commentary. He was like your next door neighbour's grandfather—the one who's always telling corny jokes—but he made one little girl's day when he produced a loonie from behind her ear and gave it to her. "Is it for me?" she asked. "Whee!"

A pair of hip-hop poets were duelling with rhymes, the crotches of their shorts down almost to their knees, their hair covered in 'do-rags. The boys' whiteness suggested to me that they too were locals—but I couldn't be absolutely sure: they certainly had the MTV gestures down pat. It struck me as interesting that urban culture should have reached into the wilds of rural Ontario: these kids, and several in their audience, dressed as if they were refugees from Jane and Finch in downtown Toronto.

Members of a Peterborough dojo were demonstrating Hap Ki Do, a martial art I'd never seen before. One young fellow put on an impressive solo display with a series of aerial kicks aimed at a punching bag. He was skinny and no more than about five feet six, but I suspect that a number of the larger boys watching him could see that this fellow wasn't someone they'd want to tangle with.

I heard a sweet, powerfully intoxicating voice some distance away, and followed it, as did a good many other folk, to find a buxom lass of about nineteen singing in front of the drugstore. Her voice was the one I'd heard the previous evening, and I was delighted to see its owner. She sang three songs *a capella*, and when she was finished a number of us moved forward to put some change into the hat she'd put down in front of her.

After several people had complimented her, I stepped up for a brief word. "I heard you singing last night," I said.

"Oh, God, I hope I didn't wake you," she said. "I know it was late."

"You did wake me, but you made waking up worthwhile," I said. "You could sing professionally, you know."

"Thank you," she said. "That's my dream."

"My name is Paul, incidentally," I said.

"My friends call me Roo," she replied, and we shook hands. Roo had come to Lakefield to see Daz's statue, and had underestimated her accommodation costs. She was now busking to pay her bus fare back home.

"Where do you live?" I asked.

"Lennoxville," she answered. "That's in Quebec. I go to Bishop's University."

"My oldest daughter goes there," I said, and it turned out they knew each other slightly. It's a small world.

After parting from Roo, I wandered around a bit more, and saw Muriel and Michael resting on a bench across from the post office. "How's the hip, Muriel?" I asked.

"I'm fine so long as I can rest every once in a while," she said bravely. I could tell that she was in fact in pain.

"She's overdone it a bit," said her husband.

There was a hot dog cart just a few yards away, and the redheaded vendor was selling tea and coffee. "May I get you a tea?" I asked.

"That would be lovely, wouldn't it, Michael?" said Muriel.

Michael began reaching for his wallet, but I was determined to make this my treat, so I jumped up and ordered three teas. Styrofoam cups are not the best vessels for a decent cup of tea, but on this day it didn't seem to matter much: the vendor had at least known to put boiling water on top of the tea bag before adding milk. I rejoined my English friends, and we sat and drank our tea together, and watched the world go by. It felt very comfortable sitting there with them: they might almost have been my own parents transported a couple of hundred kilometres just for this occasion.

"It's a lovely day, isn't it, Michael?" said Muriel.

"Yes. Yes, it's not too bad," said Michael.

Off in the distance, I saw that a kind of impromptu parade was forming. I recognised Jennifer, the rainbow-cloaked Anglican priest from Peterborough: she was holding a wooden crucifix, but she passed it to someone, and I saw that someone was Wes, and he raised it proudly. As Jennifer and Wes began to move forward and towards us, we could see that there were already about thirty or forty people behind them, and more were joining the procession all the time. There were old folks and young folks and the reluctantly middle-aged. There were white folks and brown folks and yellow folks and black folks. I saw Desmond: he was smoking a thin reefer, but nobody seemed to mind; the one policeman in sight diplomatically averted his eyes. As Jennifer and Wes drew level with us, Jennifer dipped her hand in a little pot of water she was carrying and sprinkled it over people on either side of her: I guessed, I think correctly, that it was holy water. Suddenly Emily and Ruth came into view, marching along arm-in-arm, and waving at the bystanders. I saw Ernie—he was pushing Wheelchair Guy—and Wheelchair Guy was smiling and conducting an imaginary band. And there, in amongst all the others, was my Irish friend Eric with a dram of something in his right hand, and just behind him Miss December, looking more gorgeous than any gardener has a right to do, and on her right, rather mysteriously, my friend Doug, his eyes cast heavenward, mumbling prayers to a whole communion of saints. In among a crowd of Hindus I saw Dina and Ashraf, and Dina was kind enough to blow me a kiss; and even as I watched I saw our generous friend from the trail, Ali Manji, a tiny Muslim among Hindus, handing Ashraf's father a cup of water, and stopping to steady the old man's arm when he paused to drink. And there, near the rear, but striding along happily, were Monique and Maxim, Maxim beaming away and clearly free of hip pain, Monique smiling too with a healthy husband at her side, and the sun overhead, and friendly faces all around—faces whose good will spoke (and speaks) a universal language.

I knew there would be time to chase after Monique and Maxim and bring them back to meet Michael and Muriel. And I knew, somehow, that I'd be seeing all my other friends

ACKNOWLEDGEMENTS

My warm thanks to Steven Silver, a friend of many years, and to Wayne Tefs, my good-humoured, sharp-eyed and generous editor at Turnstone.

The following are books I've found inspiring or useful as I approached this project:

Bryson, Bill. *Notes from a Small Island*. New York: William & Morrow, 1995.

Dillard, Annie. *Holy the Firm*. Toronto: Fitzhenry & Whiteside, 1998.

Gallagher, Winifred. *Spiritual Genius: 10 Masters and the Quest for Meaning*. Toronto: Random House of Canada, 2002.

Mahoney, Rosemary. *The Singular Pilgrim: Travels on Sacred Ground*. Boston: Houghton Mifflin Company, 2003.

O'Reilly, James and O'Reilly, Sean (Editors). *The Spiritual Gifts of Travel: The Best of Travelers' Tales*. San Francisco: Travelers' Tales, 2002.

Wallerstein, Judith S. *The Unexpected Legacy of Divorce: A 25 Year Landmark Study*. New York: Hyperion, 2000.

Yancey, Philip. *Soul Survivor: How My Faith Survived the Church*. Toronto: Doubleday, 2001.

Yancey, Philip. *What's So Amazing about Grace?* Grand Rapids: Zondervan, 1997.